Lint Head

Lint Head

Bill Fortenberry

St. Matthew's Press
Rome, GA

St. Matthew's Press Rome, Georgia
Copyright © 2024 Bill Fortenberry
Print ISBN 979-8-218-41444-3

This is a work of fiction. Names, characters, places and incidents either are the product of the author's imagination or are used fictitiously, and any resemblance to actual persons, living or dead, businesses, companies, events or locales is entirely coincidental.

For my family, Lisa, Ethan and Autumn. They give me love, strength and the space to create. They inspire me by their own creativity.

For Mark Batterson, whose book, *The Circle Maker*, challenged me to awaken the dream I had long put to sleep.

and

For Haley, who encouraged me to take this leap.

TABLE OF CONTENTS

1. SATURDAY MORNING, 1982
2. THAT SAINT MISS EDNA
3. THE BEAUTY SHOP GIRLS
4. WEDDING CRASHERS
5. PAUL HARVEY ON THE RADIO
6. MEET CURTIS WHITFIELD
7. LIFE IN SUMNER
8. FIRST KISS, 1956
9. IT HAPPENED AT THE WORLD'S FAIR
10. SUITCASE PACKED
11. GATLINBURG, TENNESSEE, 1982
12. INVITATION TO KNOXVILLE
13. A TRIP UP HIGHWAY 53
14. EUBANKS COUNTY HOSPITAL
15. HOME WHERE I BELONG
16. LEROY AND VIOLA
17. HENRY
18. MEET ROBERT BRANCH
19. MEET ED EARL BRANCH
20. BRENDA LEE BRANCH
21. COOKING AND CONJURING
22. LORDS AND LADIES
23. SMOKEY MOUNTAIN TEARS
24. SUNDAY MORNING SERVICE
25. INDEPENDENCE DAY
26. THE BRANCH FAMILY SECRET
27. ORDER OF THE EASTERN STAR, 1965
28. MAMA'S YELLOW APRON, 1965
29. A NEW SEASON, 1982
30. HOMECOMING
31. HAIRSPRAY AND SOUTHERN LIVING
32. FLIPPING THE MATTRESS
33. HAMBURGER AND FRENCH FRIES

I grew up extremely poor in a small Southern town. With no money to pay for college, I took a small scholarship I received and used it to pay for a six-month cosmetology course. The goal was to cut and style hair to pay my way through college.

I finished the course and secured my professional license. For the next 10 years, I cut, colored and styled hair professionally off and on. It was my work in those shops and salons that inspired *Lint Head* and the Lord and Ladies Beauty Shop.

It's an unusual career start to be sure, but one I wouldn't trade for anything in the world.

CHAPTER 1

SATURDAY MORNING, 1982

From all appearances, Brenda Branch's Saturday morning began like she had started almost every other Saturday morning for the past 26 years. She slid her still-tired feet off the edge of the bed and pointed her toes toward the quilted terry cloth Isotoners she favored. The well-worn house shoes were not as soft or as cushiony as they had been when she first got them for Christmas a decade or so ago, but they were a welcome relief from the hard-soled lace-ups she had worn every weekday since she had graduated high school back in 1956. Cotton mills are hard places, and a girl needs a good, long-lasting shoe when she's doing that kind of work, even if her feet rebelled against them.

Brenda wiggled her feet into the once cream-colored slippers and shuffled her way toward the kitchen. She pulled out the drawer that held dish towels and her apron. Like her house shoes, the carefully folded apron had faded with the years, but she would use no other. Miss Edna had given her a new one for Christmas a few years back, but Brenda had never used it. The faded yellow apron was dotted with pale pink roses printed in a delicate pattern, a treasured gift from her mama, *God rest her soul*. Brenda pulled the cast iron skillet from the shallow drawer beneath the oven and grabbed eggs, sausage and fatback from the refrigerator. The ancient Philco had manned the same corner of the kitchen for four decades. There were newer, fancier options at Sears, but her daddy didn't see a need to replace it.

"The food's cold and the ice is froze, ain't it?" her daddy had said when Brenda pointed out a side-by-side model she had seen advertised in the *News-Tribune*. Not much had changed in the Branch's kitchen since Viola Branch had died. The beadboard walls, yellowed from decades of cooking with unvented natural gas, framed a room that was both utilitarian and a memorial to the woman who had been the heartbeat of the house.

With the ingredients on the counter, Brenda commenced to cooking. It was the exact same breakfast she had cooked ever since her mama had died. How many years ago? She wasn't sure. She had blocked out that memory, and she couldn't remember without counting back through the years. *It has to be at least fifteen years, don't it?* Saddened by the thought, Brenda shifted her gaze toward the stained ceiling, also beadboard. *I sure do miss you, Mama,* Brenda thought to herself.

After her mama died, Brenda had become the woman of the house, cooking, cleaning, buying groceries, washing clothes, you name it. She disliked laundry the most. Washing and hanging a week's worth of blue jeans for herself *and* her brother was like rubbing salt in an open wound. The jeans she washed and line-dried were sewn from the very same denim she and her brother produced on their 7 a.m. to 3 p.m. shift at the mill. Three generations of Branch family members had made denim and worn it every workday of their lives, and Brenda had washed it and worn it week after week after week for more than half her life.

Over the years Brenda's days had become as monotonous as the continual whir of the spools, carders and looms that produced the denim she made, wore and laundered, but she didn't notice, at least not most days.

"Don't you ever get tired of the same ol' thing?" her friend Rogene had once asked.

"No, not really," Brenda replied. "I like knowin' what's going to happen tomorrow, and planning a grocery list is easy when you know what you have to make the whole week."

Rogene could not imagine working in a cotton mill, especially for more than half a lifetime.

"Don't those machines get on your nerves?" Rogene asked.

"Well, they did at first, but I got used to 'em."

"And all that blue cloth, don't you get tired of seeing it, not to mention *wearing* it?"

Brenda laughed. "Lord, no! I mean, I guess I might sometime, but I'm thankful to have a job, and blue jeans is the best material to work in. They don't get ruined at the mill, and they don't hardly ever wear out. Why, the last time I had to buy a pair was because I had gained weight, not because they had holes in 'em!"

Rogene shook her head.

"I just don't know how you do it."

"I wouldn't know what else to do," Brenda said matter-of-factly.

So, just as she knew that she'd wear denim and be at the mill a few minutes before 7 Monday through Friday, it was eggs, fatback, sausage and buttermilk biscuits for breakfast. Neither her daddy, who had retired from the West Oaks cotton mill, nor Robert, her brother, would go for oatmeal or cereal and milk. Once, Brenda had cooked up a box of Cream of Wheat thinking she'd try to mix things up a bit, but the intolerable complaining that came from her never-married brother and the muttering of her aging daddy ended that idea. She threw the Cream of Wheat in the trash, not even bothering to taste it for herself. *Eggs, fatback, sausage and biscuits. Every. Single. Day,* she had thought to herself that day. *You'd think they'd like to try something different ever now and then.*

The thought caused a tinge guilt to rush into her brain. She knew the Good Lord expected a woman to take care of the men in her life, even if those men are your brother and your daddy, not to mention that her mama would have wanted it that way. But today was different. *If I had some Cream of Wheat, I just might've made it today,* she thought to herself. June 5,1982 was special, and the only person who knew just how special it was, was Brenda Lee Branch.

After breakfast, served to her brother and daddy at the kitchen table, Brenda cleaned up the kitchen, wiped down the skillet, folded her mama's yellow apron and carefully placed it back in its drawer. Those chores done, she went to the bedroom to dress, stepping into her favorite pink polyester pants, the kind with the crease woven right into fabric. The elastic waist snapped around her thickening middle. She did not wear pantyhose. She always had a pair to wear with her church dresses, but the beauty of wearing pants was that you didn't have to wear hose under them. Nobody would be the wiser, and Brenda wouldn't feel like her circulation was being cut off. She buttoned up her favorite blouse, admiring the little pink rosebud pattern that covered the sleeveless top. The blouse was cream colored, like her favorite house shoes. She loved the little pink roses. They reminded her of her mama. So, outside of her house shoes and apron, she reserved pink for special occasions and for church. Pink had no place in the West Oaks cotton mill. It would just get ruined, stained by the same shade of indigo as the lint in her fuzzy, shellacked hair. You didn't have a choice but turn blue when you worked in the mill. She'd never admit it to a soul, but there were days when she checked the water in the toilet to see if her pee was blue. It never was, but it wouldn't have surprised her to find that it was.

  Brenda grabbed her saddle brown pocketbook, walked to the front door and looked through the dirty glass toward the street. Every house in the mill village had the same front door: white with the upper half a single pane of glass. Every door as covered by a screen door of some sorts. Some, like Brenda's, were the old-fashioned wooden kind that groaned open and slammed shut, powered by a rusty, tightly wound spring. Some of the houses had doors made of aluminum that eased shut with a hydraulic closer. Brenda wasn't sure she liked those doors. She didn't like the cold metal on her hand, and she didn't like the chalky metal finish. Plus, she thought she'd miss the familiar sound of a spring in tension.

Brenda sat in the metal glider on the front porch. It faced the street, making it easy to say "hey" to neighbors, watch their kids ride their bicycles, or wait for the mailman when she was expecting something special like a Christmas card. From the glider, she could see Miss Edna approaching. The creaky porch seat had once been teal and cream, but now, like so many things in Brenda's life, it had aged and faded to a dull beige and an anemic blue. She hadn't noticed the change. The glider was familiar, and, like the trusty refrigerator, it served its purpose just fine. That's what her daddy said. *You can't argue with that,* Brenda figured.

Miss Edna would be by in a few minutes. Today was beauty shop day, and Brenda and Miss Edna always went together. Miss Edna didn't mind driving for the two of them. She and Brenda worked together at the mill, and Brenda's house in the West Oaks mill village was on the way to the shop. Plus, Brenda had never learned to drive, a deficit that forced her to depend on the kindness of others or the few dollars she could scrape up every now and then to pay someone to take her where she needed to go.

Brenda had driven exactly one time before. Her daddy, Leroy, had an old International truck he had been working on. Robert and Ed Earl, Brenda's younger brother, were gone, so Leroy called Brenda outside to sit in the driver's seat and try to crank it while he fiddled under the hood. Her daddy's request had thrilled her to no end. She practically skipped to the truck.

"Look here, this is a stick shift. You're gonna have to mash the clutch and pump the gas at the same time," her daddy told her.

Brenda grinned, nodded and jumped behind the steering wheel. She could barely sit still while she waited for Leroy's instructions. Her leg jumped like a Mexican jumping bean.

"OK, try it. Try it. Go ahead, Brenda Lee, try it."

"Uh, Daddy? Which one is the clutch?"

Her daddy took his cap off and scratched his head. He walked over to the open truck door and pointed out each pedal and explained what they did. Brenda nodded and grinned from ear to ear. Her daddy walked back to the front of the truck. She couldn't see him with the hood up. So, she waited for him to tell her what to do.

"OK, you got the clutch in?"

"Yes sir!"

"You got your foot on the gas?"

"Yes sir!"

"OK try it."

Brenda turned the key in the ignition, and the truck sputtered to life.

"OK, now take your foot off the clutch."

Brenda tried to release the pressure on the pedal slowly as her daddy had instructed, but the excited quiver of her left leg caused the truck to lurch forward, knocking her daddy to the ground before going dead.

"Dammit! Brenda Lee, you 'bout killed me!" Leroy said.

"Must've forgot the damn parking brake," he muttered under his breath.

Brenda jumped out of the truck and ran around to the front. She was white as a ghost. Her daddy was still on the ground. She ran into the house crying and didn't come out of her bedroom until her mama called her down for supper.

Her daddy and two brothers laughed about the truck incident around the kitchen table that night, but she didn't find it funny. It had terrified her. Her mama tried to shush their jokes, but Leroy and his sons did not understand then just how fragile Brenda was. She couldn't process their humor.

Like a bruise that won't heal or a nagging migraine that returns every month or so, the story of how she had nearly run over her daddy lived on, perpetuated by her older brother. The incident – and its repeated telling – had left a scar, somewhere deep inside.

She never got behind a steering wheel again.

Once, several years after she had graduated high school and started working at the mill, Brenda thought she might be brave enough to try driving again. She brought up the idea to her daddy and Robert. Ed Earl, her younger brother, had married and starting a family of his own.

"Cars are smaller now," Brenda reasoned. "It ain't like I'd be driving that big ol' truck you made me crank."

"Brenda, you liked to have killed me the first time, you think I'm gonna let you drive a second time?" Leroy told his daughter. The words stung.

"Now Daddy, you know that wasn't my fault! Mama always said my legs were too short to work the clutch in your truck. I'm bigger now, and reachin' pedals ain't no problem no more."

"You ain't got no business driving," Robert said. She knew Robert would have something to say about her idea. He always did when it involved Brenda trying something new. "I take you to work and McHenry's when you need to go, and if I can't Miss Edna will."

Brenda was momentarily disappointed by their reaction, but she quickly recovered.

If I drove, we'd have to buy another car, and we don't need to be spendin' money on a car, she thought to herself. *And I do love to ride with Miss Edna. If I drove, I reckon I'd have to go places by myself. Besides, cars can be dangerous.*

She never asked again. She had a ride when she needed one, and truth be told she didn't have anywhere to go anyway.

CHAPTER 2

THAT SAINT MISS EDNA

Miss Edna pulled her burgundy-colored Buick up to the end of the sidewalk and waited. She never blew the horn or called out. She knew Brenda would be ready, even on the days she wasn't already sitting outside on the porch. Miss Edna would sit in her idling vehicle, listening to the radio, until Brenda noticed her.

Miss Edna Garmany was about as close to a saint as you'd find anywhere. She drove Brenda to and from the beauty shop every Saturday, but she helped in other ways, too. When Robert wouldn't take his sister to the grocery store, Miss Edna volunteered to drive her. Sometimes, when it was close to Christmas or Easter, Miss Edna and Brenda would go shopping at the J.C. Penney in the mall up in Paris. Belk's was a little too rich for Brenda's blood.

The mall was as fancy a place as just about anybody in Sumner or Paris had ever seen. There was a handful of folks who had been shopping in Atlanta, but they were few and far between. A passenger train used to run from Paris to Atlanta. Back in the 50s and 60s, people would get all dressed up, board the train at the depot and ride the 60 or so miles to the big city to shop at Rich's. Neither Brenda nor Miss Edna had ever done that. When the train stopped running, Paris seemed to stop growing. A new interstate highway bypassed Paris by a good 25 miles. Once people and commerce started using it, Paris was relegated to wallflower status, while the towns with interstate exits seemed to get courted by a host of suitors. A developer put up the mall after the train stopped running. It brought a few new shopping options to town, but mostly all it did was move the good stores off Broad Street to its climate-controlled promenade.

The Parisienne Mall quickly became the center of commerce in Eubanks County. The old guard family-owned stores that carried locally famous names closed, and the dark and moody mall, with J.C. Penney at one end and Belk Rhodes at the other, drew in the shoppers that had previously supported locally owned businesses. It was as nice a place as anybody could want, Brenda thought. There was a fountain right in the middle that sprayed water into a square tiled pool and all kinds of stores inside. You could get all your

Christmas shopping done right there and never get wet! It even had a picture show in it.

Brenda gasped with excitement every time she entered the mall.

"Ain't it just beautiful?" she would say to Miss Edna, who smiled weakly and nodded in response. She preferred Broad Street and the old stores, where the help wasn't a bunch of inpatient teen-agers and the lighting was bright enough to tell black from navy.

Miss Edna would stand patiently with Brenda on those shopping trips, no matter how slowly Brenda moved. Brenda loved going to Penney's. The store had good discounts, she always pointed out. Plus, they had pretty, boxed-gift sets that made real nice presents. Last Easter, Brenda found a yellow dress for herself, belt included, for just $14.99. She still had to pay tax, but even then, Brenda was able to pay without using one of the few $20 bills in her pocketbook. She didn't like giving 20s. It bothered her when then the salesgirl handed her the change. She liked her change to be counted back to her to make sure she got back what she was due, but perky salesgirls had quit doing that. Ever since the stores had stopped the practice, Brenda paid with exact change, no matter how long it took. She would rummage through her brown vinyl snap purse to get the exact number of quarters, nickels, dimes and pennies she needed. Sometimes, she'd lose count and have to start over, but it didn't matter to Brenda. She was an exact change kind of woman. She wouldn't have minded having a half dollar every now and then to help with the counting, but they were hard to come by. She now made sure to never run out of coins. Never.

"You can't count on those girls to give you the right money back," Brenda had explained to Miss Edna one day.

Miss Edna just smiled at her friend.

Brenda based her statement on a single incident two Christmases ago. She'd bought Ed Earl a cologne set that included aftershave, soap on a rope and small amber bottle of cologne. It cost exactly $7.27 with tax included. Brenda did not have a $10 bill, so she gave the cashier a $20 bill and two pennies. The salesgirl tried to give her 12 dollars and 73 cents back.

"That ain't right," Brenda told her.

"Ma'am?"

"That ain't right. I gave you twenty dollars and two cents 'cause I didn't have a 10."

"Yes ma'am."

"My change should be twelve dollars and seventy-five cents."

"What?" The girl looked disinterested and in a hurry.

"My change shoulda been twelve dollars and seventy-five cents. You see, twenty oh two minus seven twenty-seven equals twelve seventy-five."

"Why did you give me two pennies?"

"Land's sake!" Brenda didn't claim to be the sharpest tack in the box, but these young people couldn't even do simple math. "Because I didn't need any more pennies in my purse. I gave you two pennies so you could give me back three quarters, or a half-dollar and quarter if you have it."

"Ma'am?"

Brenda took a deep breath.

"Look here. You gave me twelve dollars and seventy-three cents in change, but you owed me twelve dollars and seventy-five cents on account of me giving you two pennies.

"What do you want me to do?" the cashier asked.

"I want you to take back twenty-three cents and give me a quarter."

"I can't just give you a quarter."

"I ain't asking you to," Brenda said, her patience wearing thin. "I gave you twenty oh-two, you owed me twelve seventy-five back. You gave me twelve seventy-three. You owe me two pennies."

"Okay," the salesgirl said, sliding two pennies out of the drawer for Brenda.

"I don't want two pennies!" Brenda said, her voice shrill.

"Ma'am, you just said I owe you two pennies..."

"You do. I want you to take back the twenty-three cents you gave me and give me a quarter in return. That'll make it right," Brenda said, sliding the two dimes and three pennies across the counter.

"Ma'am, I can't give you a quarter for twenty-three cents. My cash drawer will be off tonight if I do."

"Honey, your cash drawer is gonna be a mess any ways. Why don't you just call your manager over here?" Brenda's face was red. Her hands were shaking.

Recognizing that the situation was not improving and still confused by Brenda's request, the Penney's girl fished a quarter out of the cash drawer, added it to Brenda's earlier offering, and slid the coins back across the counter.

"Next, please," she called out to the person behind Brenda.

"I can't take that!" Brenda said. "If you give me twenty-five cents now, I'm gonna be stealing," Brenda was now yelling. "I ain't a thief!"

Miss Edna moved in.

"It's OK, Hon. Take the quarter," Miss Edna told her. "You know these kids are doing new math these days."

Miss Edna often used "Hon" when addressing Brenda, and Brenda liked it. It was a term her mama had used often, short for honey and just as sweet.

But the extra quarter in Brenda's hand bothered her. She gripped it tight until she saw the mall fountain. She had heard that they clean the coins out of the fountain and donate the money to charity every so often. She figured her twenty-three cents could go there, and the good Lord would be okay with that. She stopped squarely in front of the tiled fountain and chucked the coins into the water. Only then could she go about the rest of her day.

Miss Edna's Job-like patience carried over into many of her interactions with Brenda, but she didn't mind. She ate lunch with Brenda at the mill and, when she could, she would drive Brenda to doctor's appointments or church. She always bought Brenda a card on her birthday, and she always gave her a little gift at Christmas. Miss Edna was enough older than Brenda that she could have been her mama, and, truth be told, Brenda sometimes thought of her that way, though she would never say that out loud to her. *That just wouldn't be right.* As for Miss Edna, well, she felt sorry for Brenda, as sorry for her as she was for a lost child or an abandoned puppy. She once wondered aloud whether her purpose on earth was to help take care of Brenda, even though she had a daughter of her own.

The commercial jingle on the radio in Miss Edna's Buick nudged Brenda's attention. She looked up, waved at Miss Edna, grabbed her purse and trotted down the sidewalk to the gate. She loved these regular Saturday trips to the beauty shop. They provided a brief escape from her predictable world and a glimpse into a side of life she'd only heard of there and in the breakroom at work.

As she opened the front passenger door, Brenda heard the familiar opening to Swap Shop.

"Must be 9:30!" Brenda said with far more animation than the sentence required. You could set your clock by that radio station. Swap Shop always came on exactly at 9:30 on Saturday mornings, and she and Miss Edna always listened in on their way to the beauty shop.

They both liked to listen to Mike, the host. He had a friendly, comforting voice, and, on top of that, you never knew what kind of deal you might find or what sort of codger might call in.

"Hey Mike, this is Grover. I've got half a can of ceiling paint, a washing machine motor and a sling blade if anybody needs 'em."

Mike asked Grover if he had anything he was looking for.

"Well, yeah, there is. I need a dipstick for a 1964 Ford Falcon if anybody's got one. They can call me."

Grover gave the radio listeners his phone number.

It was okay if you missed the phone number. Mike kept a running list of the things people were looking for and the things people had to give away, and he always wrote the phone number down beside them.

There had been a couple of times when Mike had really saved the day.

Once, there was a lady looking for a wheelchair for her husband who had just had a stroke. She called Swap Shop. Mike had thought she just sounded real pitiful and wanted to help. He remembered that a caller the week before had a wheelchair they were looking to get rid of. Mike connected the wheelchair owner with the wheelchair seeker, making four very happy people, if you include Mike.

"That, ladies and gentlemen, is the beauty of radio," a choked-up Mike told his listeners the following Saturday morning. You could tell from his voice that he was crying just a little bit.

"You have or need anything else, Grover?"

With Grover taken care of, Mike answered the next call.

"We could use that paint," Brenda said, staring ahead. "There's a brown circle on the kitchen ceiling from that roof leak last year."

"Did you write down the number?" Miss Edna asked.

"No. Maybe I'll call Mike later and get it."

Brenda wouldn't call. Neither Miss Edna nor Brenda had ever swapped for anything on Swap Shop, but Mike's familiar voice and the hoard of treasures traded on the show always gave them something to talk about on Saturday mornings.

CHAPTER 3

THE BEAUTY SHOP GIRLS

It was 1982, but entering the Lords and Ladies Beauty and Barber Shop was like walking into an underlit time machine where everything was the color of mustard. Yellowed, fake wood paneling, harvest gold Formica countertops and a linoleum floor the color of overripe bananas gave every face reflected in the plate glass mirrors a hint of jaundice. Hooded hair dryers covered in Dijon-colored Naugahyde lined the back wall, only adding to the sickly presentation, their hot air circulating a combination of hydrogen peroxide, ammonia, apple shampoo and hairspray.

At the shop, the girls were in rare form.

"You ain't holdin' yer mouth right," said Tally, the owner.

Jane Ellen's desire to become a platinum blond was stuck somewhere between the linoleum and an Easter chick, eliciting Tally's commentary.

"I want it to look natural, Earlene," Jane Ellen had told her stylist.

That was asking a lot.

Earlene had managed to lighten Jane Ellen's normally dark hair to its current state, but every eye in the shop was aware that Earlene had more work to do. If Earlene was going to get her client's hair to Marilyn Monroe, it was going to take more bleach, more peroxide, holding her mouth right and a touch from Jesus.

"Don't worry about it, Honey," Earlene said, after a quick, silent prayer. "We'll get it fixed. We're gonna pull it through a frosting cap, put some more high-powered bleach on it and set you under a dryer. Then, when we're done, we're gonna put a toner on it."

Jane Ellen's request to be a blonde was inspired from her escapades the previous night. She had gone to the Fuzzy Duck Friday night and was providing a play-by-play in between trips to the sink and the hair dryer.

The Fuzzy Duck hadn't been open all that long. People in Eubanks County talked about the nightclub like it had been the inspiration for *Urban Cowboy*. It was not. Nobody ever stayed until the lights came on, but if they had, they would have run for the hills. Behind the dim lights, neon and thick haze of cigarette smoke was a poor man's honkytonk set up in an abandoned Big Star grocery store. Nevertheless, plenty of folks drove over to Fort Payne to kick up their heels to "Amos Moses" and drink long-necks.

"I even tried one of them Sex on the Beaches and a sloe gin fizz!" Jane Ellen said.

The mention of sex caught Brenda's ear. She let out a high-pitched "Whoop!" followed by "OH MY LORD!" The Messiah's name was pronounced in two syllables: "low-word" – not uncommon in little Sumner, Georgia. She and Miss Edna had arrived at the beauty shop in the middle of Jane Ellen's story.

Walking in the door at Lords and Ladies was like walking into a beehive. Wands curled and combs flew, engulfed in a cloud of hair spray and accompanied by the constant roar of hair dryers and conversation. Outside of church, this was the most social part of Brenda's week. Her sheltered life led to a tendency to interject her own voice into other people's conversations, or to exclaim in reaction to something she overheard that wasn't meant for her ears.

The noise and the slight hearing loss that had resulted from years of working at the mill had gotten Brenda into the habit of speaking too loudly – with one exception. When discussing her own medical issues. Brenda always whispered medical terms or references to them.

A couple of years back, Brenda had a complete hysterectomy. She recovered from the surgery without complication, but to Brenda, it had been a life-altering experience. Ever since then, she talked about it often and always with her peculiar volume change.

"Hey Teresa!" Brenda said. "Whoowee! I know my hair needs something today. Lord, it's growed like a weed, and it's full of lint. It's growed like that ever since my ..."

Brenda finished her sentence in a barely audible whisper, "*surgery.*"

"Honey, did you say you had surgery?"

"Yes, I did!" Brenda said, again louder than necessary.

"What kind of surgery did you have, Sugar? I hope everything's OK."

"I had *female surgery*," Brenda replied, whispering only the last two words.

Teresa patted her customer on the shoulder.

"My goodness, precious!" Teresa said. "I thought you meant you'd had *another* surgery."

Brenda shook her head. "Did you ever have *female surgery?"* she asked Teresa, again ending in a whisper.

Teresa nodded.

"Girl, I had all my parts taken out. Best decision I ever made, outside of divorcing my second husband." She chuckled.

"Whoop!" Brenda exclaimed. "I reckon I'll see if it helps me."

Brenda's exclamations of "Whoop!" also were jolting, especially in contrast to her whispered medical words. They caused her stylist to yank her hair, which elicited another "Whoop!" from Brenda. This, too, was a peculiarity of Brenda's. It seemed to have no origin or explanation. The folks who knew her had just come to expect an occasional "whoop" from Brenda.

At the shop, there was no covering Brenda's intrigue and shock at Jane Ellen's Fuzzy Duck narration. Brenda's thoughts were racing: *Women was drinking. They was drinking alcohol ... in the open. They was drinking ... and dancing. And to beat it all, they was dancing with strange men they didn't even know! What was the world coming to?* Truth be known, Brenda secretly wondered what it might be like to go dancing and drink a slow fizzing drink like, *what did she call it? Sex on the Beach? Well, not that. Definitely not that!* She could NEVER bring herself to order something that had the word sex in it. Brenda wasn't sure if she'd ever said that word out loud, though she might have whispered it once. Still, she might consider ordering one of those wine coolers she had heard about, as long as her daddy and Robert didn't find out – Miss Edna either. She probably wouldn't approve of wine coolers.

Somewhere in the shop, Juanita Turner had just mentioned that she had returned from the beach. It was a private conversation with her hairdresser, Mae, but Brenda didn't seem to realize that.

"Y'all went to Panama City Beach?" Brenda interjected, tossing the words over her right shoulder. "We went to the beach one time," Brenda continued loudly. "Daddy drove us all to Tybee Island. We ate fried baloney sandwiches with mustard, drank Double Cola and even stopped at a café on the way back to get a milkshake. Can y'all believe it? We stopped at a café! I got a chocolate milkshake. Well, me and mama shared it, but we had the best time. Do you remember me telling you about that Miss Edna? We had the best time. Daddy let us get out of the car and put our toes in the water before we had to get back in. We sat there in the parking lot watching that water while we ate our sandwiches. All the windows was down, so you could feel the breeze."

Brenda's mind took a mid-story jump.

"Hey, did y'all know the World's Fair was in Knoxville. The WORLD'S FAIR! In Knoxville, Tennessee!" She emphasized the first syllable of the state's name instead of the last. "I bet they have all kinds of food there…"

Brenda caught herself. Her face flushed crimson. She had almost said too much. She stopped talking, not saying much of anything for the rest of her appointment.

Tally and the girls just shook their heads. You never knew what Brenda might say, so they usually just went with it.

Brenda sat quietly, smiling to herself every once in a while, while Teresa finished styling her hair, teasing each curl into submission before fanning it out, laying it down and nudging it into place. The girls at the shop didn't pay her too much attention anyway. Not that it mattered. The Mullinax widows were there for their usual 10:30 appointment, and they were pretty good at commanding nearly everyone's attention. The sisters-in-law started talking from the minute they got in the car together and carried on the conversation without missing a beat, regardless of where they were. They hollered their discussions at each other from beneath the dryers heating their rolled-up hair and turning their ears bright pink. It didn't matter to the Mullinaxes that others were talking in the tiny shop. They just talked louder. Race days at Talladega were quieter.

"How much corn did you get?" Peg yelled.

"Silver Queen." Pat hollered back.

"How *much*?"

"Two fifty a bushel!"

"Pat! How *much* did you *buy*?"

"Half a bushel. That'll be enough, don't you think?"

Their conversation continued the entire 30 minutes the yellowing plastic domes covered their heads. Thank the Lord, neither felt the need to update the other on her ongoing health problems this week, Miss Edna thought. Those discussions could go places nobody, except maybe Brenda, wanted to go.

Back in their chairs, waiting for Tally and Teresa to comb their hair out, the Mullinax girls failed at an attempt to drop their voices, having caught the tail end of Jane Ellen's narration of her scandalous weekend.

"Tally, did she say she was dancing on top of the speakers?"

Tally giggled and shushed her client.

"There ain't no beach in Fort Payne, what's this nonsense about Jane Ellen having sexual relations on some beach?"

Teresa turned her head, covered her mouth and walked away. She could barely keep herself together. A few deep breaths later, she had regained her composure enough to offer an explanation to the Mullinax in-laws. Teresa explained the liquor drinks to Pat, who found the information only slightly less scandalous.

"Why in the world would you name a drink something like that?" Pat asked, loudly "There ain't nothing good that can come from drinking something with that kind of name. You might as well be standing on a street corner and selling yourself like a Jezebel."

Teresa lowered her head down to her client's ear to remind her that Jane Ellen was within hearing distance, but Pat didn't care, and neither did Jane Ellen. She took the gossip as fuel and was having the time of her life embellishing her already shocking story.

Though she'd never admit it to a living soul, Jane Ellen was Brenda Lee's hero, at least in this moment. Brenda had hung on to every colorful word, smiling when Jane Ellen smiled, laughing when she laughed, and blushing when Jane Ellen mentioned dancing with men she hardly knew.

CHAPTER 4
WEDDING CRASHERS

For two decades and more, Brenda's life had seldom veered from its routine. Eggs, fatback, sausage and biscuits for breakfast. Work at the mill five days a week. A baloney sandwich and Ruffles potato chips for lunch. Church on Wednesday nights and twice on Sundays. Beauty shop appointment on Saturday mornings.

Since Brenda didn't drive, some things were out of her control. Grocery shopping could happen just about any time on a Saturday. There was no time, and she was too tired to shop during the week. Sometimes she went with Miss Edna, if Miss Edna was going. Sometimes she had to depend on Robert or her daddy to take her. She'd rather go with Miss Edna. *Miss Edna wasn't impatient like the men*, she'd thought to herself at least a hundred times.

Going to the grocery store with her daddy or brother made Brenda nervous. *They don't want to go in the first place, even though I make sure to buy their favorites, shop the sales and always make sure we have plenty of food at the house, but that don't seem to matter.* Both Leroy and Robert would sit in the car while she got the groceries, and that made her feel rushed. She was afraid that in her hurry to get done, she would miss out on the best deals or forget something, even though she rarely did. Brenda used a list to help her remember everything she needed, but if the store ever moved things around or she felt like she was taking too much time, the list didn't help. Plus, she liked to take her time picking out fruit and vegetables. That was not something you could rush. She thumped every melon, tested every tomato and inspected every banana before making her decision. In shopping for canned goods, she checked every expiration date and every price. Buying groceries wasn't so much about nutrition as it was saving money and making what she did buy last as long as she could. *They think I was born yesterday. But I wasn't,* she thought to herself. *Five for a dollar ain't a better deal than 19 cents a can. I didn't graduate high school for nothing! It's like they think I can't do simple math!*

The one, blessed (she pronounced the word in two syllables, "bless-ed") exception to Brenda's Saturday routine was wedding days.

A few years ago, a girl Brenda worked with, Rogene Caldwell, figured out a way that allowed her and Brenda to experience the fancier side of life. Rogene is in her 30s and Brenda is past 40, but at the mill, you hardly ever called a female "woman". "Woman" was too harsh. Mill women call each other girl, no matter their ages. Except maybe Miss Edna. Miss Edna commanded respect from the mill girls. They always called her Miss Edna.

Unlike Brenda, Rogene didn't go to church on Sundays. While Brenda was spending time with the Lord, singing *Bringing in the Sheaves* or listening to her brother preach another of his hell-fire-and-damnation sermons, Rogene was sipping a sweet, iced tea or a Coke and thumbing through the Sunday paper on the back steps of the mill house she lived in.

Mill houses in Sumner all look exactly the same. They are white, two-story duplexes with clapboard siding. A wide, rail-less porch spans the front. In front of every front door was a screen door – a requisite for Southern summers, and every porch had a tongue-and-groove ceiling that at one time had been painted a watery blue, the color of Caribbean shallows. Screen doors let air in and keep bugs out, and the haint blue ceilings keep evil away. Brenda had learned that from her mama.

"It's in the Bible, Brenda Lee," Brenda's mama once told her. "The book of Matthew says demons can't cross water. They see that blue on the porch and they pass right on by."

Brenda never understood why a demon would think a ceiling was water, but for as long as she could remember families painted their porch ceilings a shade of blue that was a straight up match to the pictures of the Gulf of Mexico she had seen. A schoolteacher once told her that haint blue ceilings were folklore handed down from old wives and conjurers, but she wasn't about to mess with it. If blue porch ceilings kept the devil away, then her porch ceilings would be blue. Out back, each house has an outbuilding that, in the days before refrigerators were common, had served as an icehouse. Now they just held lawnmowers, gas cans, shovels and sling-blades.

Rogene's favorite perch was the concrete steps centered on the front porch. She loved reading the engagement and wedding write ups in the *Life in Paris* section of the paper. Sumner didn't have a newspaper, so if a Sumner girl or boy was getting married, the engagement write-up and the wedding follow-up were printed in the Sunday *Paris News-Tribune*.

A secondary hobby of Rogene's was watching for last names that didn't seem to go together or went together comically well. She cataloged the juxtaposed names in her mind and pulled them out to enliven conversation whenever she felt the need.

"There was this on time when the Hightower girl married a boy named Critchlow; that one was pretty good," Rogene would say, "And then, oh my Lord, there was the time Miss Christmas got engaged to Mr. Garland. Christmas-Garland betrothed. Can you even believe it?"

Rogene laughed till her sides hurt when she first read that one, and when Penny Dollar had married Tommy Kountz, Rogene couldn't contain herself.

"What was that girl thinking?" Rogene hollered out loud to no one. "Her mama done named her Penny Dollar, and now she's gonna be Penny Kountz? Lord, I hope her first name's not Every!"

No matter how many times she said every Penny Kountz, Rogene would laugh so hard she would lose her breath. Her mouth would be open, her face red and her shoulders quaking, but absolutely no sound would escape her mouth. Then, when her lungs finally rebelled, her diaphragm would convulse, and she would gasp for air like a drowning victim, only to start the whole episode over again.

The notion to attend a wedding uninvited came one Sunday when Rogene read that the Treglown girl was getting married the next week. The reception was going to be down by the creek, right across from the cotton mill. The full span of Sumner wasn't more than three miles from one end to the other. The West Oaks mill was at the center of town, right beside the railroad tracks, which ran east-west alongside the mill. Silver Creek meandered through the middle of the mill property, and a rock bridge connected the north and south ends of the little hamlet. First Baptist Church had located their church building across from the mill alongside the creek, just a stone's throw away from an old brick grist mill. The grist mill was the location for the Treglown reception, and Rogene had never seen the inside of the 100-year-old building. The Treglowns were nice people. She sure did like their mama, and everybody knew their granddaddy, who sold tomatoes by the side of Maple Avenue every summer.

"Hey, I've got an idea. We should go to the reception," Rogene said to Brenda the next day at work.

"I ain't invited," Brenda said.

"I ain't either," Rogene said. "We wouldn't be going to the wedding, Brenda. We'd just be stoppin' by the reception. You know, to congratulate the happy couple."

"Whoop!" Brenda said, way too loud. "Can you even do that?"

"The invitation probably got lost," Rogene said, creating a scenario she thought Brenda would buy into. "Everybody knows the Treglowns. You know we was supposed to be invited."

Brenda did *not* know she was supposed to be invited, but going to a fancy reception at the old grist mill sure sounded like fun. It was on a Saturday. Her hair style would be fresh, and she didn't have anything else to do. There would be time to get groceries later.

"OK, I'll do it!"

The next Saturday, after Miss Edna dropped her back home. Brenda put on one of her Sunday dresses and walked out to the porch to wait on Rogene.

"Where you goin'? her brother asked.

"I'm going to a weddin'," Brenda told him. She tried to make her voice sound normal.

"Who's gettin' married?" Robert never asked follow-up questions. His reply made her realize she had made her pronouncement with a little too much sass.

"The Treglown girl," Brenda replied, with as much nonchalance as she could muster.

"Oh."

Robert went on about his business, which wasn't much of nothing. He had been rummaging around in the tool shed out back, but there wasn't much reason to. The dry, hot May had killed all the grass, and nobody had time to mess with flowers. Maybe he would patch the tear in the screen door that let the bugs in, though probably not. That tear had been there for six years.

Rogene rolled up in a rusted-out Nova with a bad muffler that announced her approach a block away. Brenda slid into the passenger seat.

"Here we go!"

"Here we go!" Brenda repeated.

The girls parked in the First Baptist Church parking lot and walked over to the grist mill. Brenda was nervous. She pulled her pocketbook close in and kept her eyes down. The pair walked right in and signed the guest book like they belonged there. Nobody said a thing to them.

Rogene called Brenda over to the food tables.

"Looky here! They've got them barbecue weenies and Jordan almonds!"

Brenda had no idea what a Jordan almond was, but it sure sounded fancy. She got herself a plate and filled it up. She got an extra scoop of the sugar-shelled almonds.

She and Rogene stood off to the side, nibbling, nodding and smiling, until the bride and groom walked in the door.

"Whoop! She's so purty!" Brenda said, louder than she should have.

A couple of people snickered, but Brenda didn't notice.

Sherry Treglown was beautiful. Well, she wasn't Sherry Treglown anymore, not after today. Oh Lord! Brenda realized that she didn't know who the groom was. That realization made her flush for a minute, but she settled down. She couldn't think about that, not when the bride was so pretty and so happy. Brenda started crying. She couldn't help herself. She opened her pocketbook and started rummaging for a Kleenex.

"Look at her!" Brenda said to Rogene. "She's like a princess!"

Sherry and her groom held hands as they entered the room. The bride was dressed all in white, of course. Her wedding gown went all the way to the floor and had layers and layers of ruffles. Her new husband had on a pale blue tuxedo with a pale blue ruffled shirt and a darker blue bowtie. He looked like James Bond, Brenda thought.

After the couple cut the cake and stuffed it into each other's faces, which made Brenda laugh out loud, she and Rogene sidled over to get a slice of the wedding cake and the groom's cake. The wedding cake was three layers and the same baby blue as the groom's tuxedo. It had pale pink roses on it that made her think of her favorite blouse. A plastic bride and groom stood on top, adding a good five or six inches to the already-tall cake. The little bride had the same color hair as Sherry. The groom's cake was about the cutest thing Brenda had ever seen. It was decorated to look like a football field, with green icing on top and white lines evenly spaced across it. There were even goal posts on each end. Best of all, it was chocolate! Brenda made sure to get a corner piece of the football cake. She wanted as much icing as she could get. Her diabetes doctor wouldn't be happy, but he would just have to accept the fact that everybody needed a little sugar every now and then.

The two stayed at the wedding reception until the very end. At the front door of the mill was a concrete bird bath filled with little sachets of blue netting tied in pale blue ribbon. Each one held a handful of rice. Rogene was ready to go after she had had a slice of wedding cake, but Brenda wanted to throw rice. So, they stayed, laughing with the invited guests as Sherry and her new husband ran to their car.

From that point on, Rogene had scoured the Sunday paper for weddings they could go to. She would tell Brenda about their options over lunch or work breaks.

"They used to go to our church," Brenda would say.

Or, Rogene might offer, "Her daddy worked at the mill."

"I believe I went to school with her mama."

"Her brother changes the oil in daddy's car."

"Don't she get her hair done at Lord and Ladies?"

Brenda loved going to weddings, to see young love blossom right before your eyes. Her favorite part was when the couple locked their elbows and tried to drink the sparkling grape juice out of tall, fancy glasses without spilling it. More than once she had gone home and practiced the move in the bathroom mirror, never sure whether the bride was drinking out of her own glass or the groom's. *Lord, I'd have to have somebody walk me through it!* Brenda also liked it when the bride threw her flowers backwards to all the single girls. One time, Brenda almost caught the flowers. *Oh Lord, they're coming straight at me!* The flowers arced perfectly in front of Brenda, but she didn't dare catch them. She let the bouquet fall to the floor at her feet and backed away, a little embarrassed that she was even standing there.

"Whoop!" she said too loud. "I don't reckon I'm getting married anytime soon."

The younger single girls around her laughed when she said it, and that made Brenda feel better.

She and Rogene had a lot of fun going to those weddings. She could only imagine what it might be like to go to her own.

Would she wear a long dress? Maybe she'd get a pretty short one like girls used to do in the 50s. She could wear a white pillbox hat with it that has that wide netting on it.

Would she have a reception? She could have it in the church fellowship hall. She had been to a reception there before. The ladies of the church had fixed it up real nice. They had screens behind the wedding cake table made out of white lattice that they stuck plastic roses in. It was about the prettiest thing she had ever seen.

The wedding cake! She didn't even know where to begin. Maybe three layers, but not with them columns in between. Those things scared her. *What if one of them layers toppled over. Lord have mercy!* Maybe she could find a bride and groom on top that looked like her and the man she loved.

Of the dozens of receptions she and Rogene attended over the years, Brenda's favorite had taken place just a few months before. Holly Wood married Frank Bush right before Christmas in 1981. There was no way Rogene was going to miss that party.

"First," she said to Brenda, "what was that mama thinking to name her baby Hollywood?" She ran the words together when she spoke them. "HOLLYWOOD! Why in the Lord's name would you do such a thing to a child? But then, to top it off, Holly's gonna marry a boy named Bush? Her new name is gonna be Holly Bush! HOLLY BUSH, and it's a CHRISTMAS wedding!"

Rogene's face was redder than a beet from laughing. Brenda laughed with her, but it really didn't strike her nearly as funny as it had Rogene. What *did* strike her fancy was going to a Christmas wedding.

Brenda had always thought of weddings as warm-weather events, June brides were as close to perfection as they could be. But the notion of a Christmas wedding just seemed, she didn't know how to put it into words…magical.

The Wood-Bush wedding was held at the First Presbyterian Church, located just outside of Sumner on the banks of Silver Creek. It was a tiny little church building with no place for a reception, but it was set on just about the prettiest piece of land you could imagine. The church was white with board and batten siding. On the red front doors were two of the prettiest Christmas wreaths Brenda had ever seen. The green magnolia circles were tied with white satin bows.

Brenda and Rogene didn't go to the wedding, but they did peek into the little church during the reception. Inside, two beautiful, flocked Christmas trees lit with clear lights and decorated in white doves and snowflakes flanked the altar. The sight of the white-decorated evergreens took Brenda's breath away.

The reception was staged under a big tent beside the church to protect the couple and their guests from the chilly weather. Rogene and Brenda walked under the white tent with their cardigans on. Christmas carols played in the background, and the tables looked like something out of *Southern Living*. The centerpieces held a mixture of red poinsettias, green rosemary Christmas trees and white candles in silver candlesticks, each tied with white satin ribbon.

"A sight to behold," Brenda whispered to Rogene.

The solid white wedding cake featured shiny holly leaves and red berries. When Brenda got her a slice of the cake, she used her fingers to remove the leaves and berries and let out a "Whoop!"

"Rogene! You won't believe it, but these leaves and berries are made out of icing of some kind! You can eat 'em!"

More Christmas trees, all decorated in white and lit with clear lights sat in each corner of the tent, casting a warm glow on the festivities. Even the food followed the theme. White mints, silver Jordan almonds. Strawberries dipped in white chocolate. Even some of the white petit fours had been dusted in silver. The coconut groom's cake had a little ice-skating pond in the middle of it. Brenda overheard somebody say the couple had gone ice skating on their first date at a place down in Atlanta. *Ice skating! That's so romantic!* Brenda thought to herself.

After the best man introduced Mr. and Mrs. Frank Bush for the first time, the couple slow danced to *White Christmas*. Brenda clutched her purse to her chest and warbled along with Bing on the last two lines.

May your days be merry and bright,
And may all your Christmases by white.

She was crying.

"It's just too much," Brenda said to Rogene. "I mean, a wedding, Christmas time and White Christmas to top it all off. I just can't hardly stand it."

At the end of the reception, an old red truck pulled up. Tied to the truck's grill was a green magnolia wreath also with a white satin bow. And, as the couple prepared to leave for their honeymoon (they were going skiing up in Boone, North Carolina!), all the guests, both invited and uninvited, lined the pathway with fake snow in their hands. Holly and

Frank held hands and walked quickly to the '49 Chevy pickup in a blizzard of white. As they drove off, the last thing the guests saw was a sign on the tailgate that said in the prettiest red writing, *And they lived happily ever after.*

"Oh, Rogene," Brenda gushed as they walked to Rogene's Nova, "wasn't that the most beautiful wedding you have ever seen in your life?"

Rogene's instinct was to reply like a cynic, but she couldn't. Holly Bush's wedding reception was a top 10 in her book, and she and Brenda had been to quite a few receptions.

Over time, the girls had eaten their weight in Swedish meatballs, chicken wings, cheese balls, Ritz crackers, ranch dip, peanuts, Jordan almonds and pillow mints at every fellowship hall, gymnasium and church yard in Sumner. Rogene was careful not to invite herself to the fancy weddings up in Paris. That would have been pushing it. But, if there was a wedding in Sumner, and there was even a remote connection to the bride, the groom, the parents or the grandparents, you could count on finding Brenda and Rogene at the reception.

CHAPTER 5
PAUL HARVEY ON THE RADIO

Her curls freshly placed, Brenda was positively blooming, even more than her blouse. She slid into the passenger seat of Miss Edna's Buick to head home from the Lords and Ladies. Thanks to Teresa's miracles with hair curlers and a teasing comb, and the promise of the day, Brenda sat a little straighter in the seat. She set her pocketbook in her lap, laced her fingers around it and smiled. Miss Edna didn't notice, and Brenda thought that was a good thing. *If Miss Edna, the beauty shop girls, Robert or daddy knew what was in my head right now, not a one of them would believe it, and I'd be in a heap of trouble.*

In the car, Paul Harvey had replaced Swap Shop. He was always good to listen to.

Paul told his listeners he was in Dallas.

"He's in Dallas, Miss Edna!"

He said his "traveling microphone" was at a radio station in the Lone Star state.

"I doubt he's in Dallas," Miss Edna said. "This is a repeat. I heard this one before."

Paul told his listeners about a local centenarian who had been asked to share her secret to such a long life.

Her secret, she said, has only two steps: 1) Avoid doctors, and 2) Avoid men.

"Whoop!" Brenda said, in response to the part about avoiding men. She didn't say anything else, thinking she'd better keep her thoughts to herself.

Miss Edna shook her head. It was a reaction to both Paul Harvey and Brenda Lee Branch. She knew what a good life was, and she was grateful that she had had a good man and a good doctor in her life.

"I just don't know that I believe that," Miss Edna said.

CHAPTER 6
MEET CURTIS WHITFIELD

The only man in Brenda's life, other than her daddy and her brothers, had made a brief, but memorable appearance years ago. That is, it had been years ago until this past Tuesday.

Tuesday's supper is always fried salmon patties, hushpuppies and carrots cooked with sugar. Leroy liked to eat his salmon patties and hush puppies in ketchup. He didn't dip a bite into the ketchup. He poured ketchup on the top of the salmon patty and on top of the hushpuppies. His mama had always served carrots with salmon, so Brenda's mama, Viola, did the same. And now, Brenda carried on the tradition.

Brenda had been frying the salmon patties when the phone rang. She wiped the grease from her hands on a worn hand towel and picked up the phone.

"Hello?" She said too loudly.

"Is this Brenda Lee Branch?" a man's voice, vaguely familiar, asked on the other end.

"Yes. Who's this speaking?" Brenda asked. It was rare for her to get phone calls, especially from a man.

"Well, Brenda Lee, I just want to tell you that you're all I've thought about for the past 27 years."

"Who is this?" Brenda asked, still too loud and obviously a little scared.

"You don't recognize me?" the voice on the other end asked.

"No, I do not!" Brenda said, an anxious fear rising in her chest. "And I think maybe I ought to hang up on you."

"Now don't do that, Brenda Lee. It's took me four months to find your number."

"Who is this, again?"

"Brenda Lee, it's Curtis Whitfield."

The blood drained out of Brenda's face. She drew in all the air her lungs would hold and started pacing back and forth as far as the loosely coiled phone cord would let her.

"Brenda Lee? Brenda Lee?"

"Uh, Curtis Whitfield. Why are you calling on me? You know I ain't allowed to talk to you."

Twenty-seven years earlier, when she was a senior in high school, Brenda had fallen hard for Curtis. He was rough around the edges, but she could excuse that. His daddy was a drunk, and his mama was as mean as a striped snake, at least that's what people said. Curtis pretty much raised himself, and he didn't do such a good job of it. With nobody to teach him right from wrong, Curtis landed more often on the wrong side of things than the right. Back then, Brenda had reasoned that all he needed was a good woman to love him and good dose of Jesus, and he'd be a good man. Afterall, it wasn't his fault that the poor boy didn't have anybody to care for him like he should've.

Curtis had blown into West Oaks High School full of attitude and grease, his shiny face pocked by acne and scars. He carried himself with a James Dean swagger. He winked at Brenda the first time she passed him in the hallway, something he continued to do whenever he saw her. Both embarrassed and flattered, Brenda would drop her head, pull her books to her chest and gain speed in response. Curtis would laugh and watch her as she walked hurriedly to class.

Curtis had carried on these brief flirtations day after day from September all the way to Christmas, and as fall quarter gave way to the winter, Brenda found herself hoping for Curtis's winks. No other boy had ever shown her that kind of attention. His winks and crooked grin made her feel...just a little special.

After Christmas, Brenda didn't see Curtis in the hallways anymore. Now, she only saw him at the corner of a building before or after school or at lunchtime. She wondered if he ever even went to class. It turned out that he did not.

By February, Brenda didn't see Curtis at school at all, and it made her sad, but she never told anybody. Every once in a while, she'd see him standing outside the filling station or leaning in the window at the drive-in café, but that just made her sadder. She doubted he saw her at all.

On June 2, 1956, Brenda walked across the stage of the West Oaks auditorium to accept her high school diploma. Brenda's mama and daddy had been proud that their only daughter was graduating, but they tempered their joy with concern. Brenda hadn't dated in high school, and the Branches didn't have the money to send their daughter to teacher's college or secretarial school like she had wanted. Her future prospects didn't look too promising. The only thing they knew to do was to take her to the mill and ask about getting her a job. The only other option for a plain girl with no money in a small town was to wait tables or find a job in Paris, and they sure as fire weren't going to do that. Working in Paris would have required a six or seven mile drive every day, and waiting tables could lead a girl to no good. No, like her brothers and her daddy before her, Brenda would take a job at the mill and be thankful for it.

Immediately following the graduation ceremony, Brenda's daddy drove toward the West Oaks mill. Nothing had changed on that route since the first time Brenda remembered her backseat view. Millhouses lined both sides of Maple. Then, as they approached the mill itself, she began to see other signs of Sumner community life: the baseball field on the left, and just a block or so up the road, the pharmacy and McHenry's Grocery Store on the right. Beside McHenry's was their destination–Bennett's Cafeteria. Across from the pharmacy-grocery-cafeteria line-up stood the mill itself: a massive, four-story expanse of red brick and arched windows. Two matching red-brick smokestacks rose above it, 10-stories tall, like the king and queen on a chess board, holding court over squares and squares of pawns.

Although the Branches couldn't do much for their daughter, they were determined to celebrate her graduation. They took her to Sumner's lone sit-down eatery. Bennett's Cafeteria was located directly across the street from the mill, making it easy for the mill bosses to walk over and eat lunch there, and convenient for families seeking a good, affordable meal close to home. Leroy parked his '46 Ford Tudor and walked ahead with Viola. Brenda trailed a few steps behind them in her white dotted Swiss dress and white shoes, swaying back and forth with a broad smile on her face. *I graduated! I can't hardly believe it!* She thought to herself, imagining the people she passed noticing her pretty dress and how smart she looked. She didn't know what the future held, but it had to be something wonderful. Brenda would have gone into full daydream mode had she not run directly into Curtis Whitfield, who was leaning against the wall just outside the grocery store.

"Brenda Lee, are you gonna talk to me? I tried all year to get you to say something to me."

Curtis drew hard on his Camel and blew the smoke out of the side of his mouth.

Brenda managed a quick and barely audible reply, "Hey, Curtis."

"Hey. Since you graduated you ought to go with me to get a milkshake tonight as a celebration."

"I...I don't think my daddy will let me."

"Aww, come on, now. You're a woman now. That piece of paper you got today practically proves it. Can't you do as you please?"

Brenda shook her head quickly. "Maybe you could come over to the house and meet my daddy."

"OK, Brenda Lee," he half chuckled. "Maybe I can."

Curtis dipped his shoulder, turned and ambled away, exhaling a trail of smoke. Brenda straightened the skirt of her dress and went inside the cafeteria.

Brenda got her tray and walked along the cafeteria line, following her daddy's lead.

"Who was that you was talking to?" Brenda's daddy asked.

"It was nobody daddy, just a boy from school," she replied.

"Well, he looks like he's up to no good. Stay away from him, you hear?" her daddy said.

Brenda kept silent.

Leroy and Viola both ordered fried chicken. Brenda didn't want fried chicken. She and mama cooked it once a week. Today was special. She wanted a hamburger. They never had hamburgers at home.

"Daddy, Can I have a hamburger patty on a bun?"

"Yes ma'am! We're celebratin'!"

Leroy and Viola ordered fried okra and corn with their chicken. Brenda ordered French fries. The West Oaks Cafeteria deep-fried their fries. Brenda thought they tasted way better than the limp, oil-laden, skillet-fried potatoes her mama sometimes cooked.

Once she and her parents settled in a vinyl booth, Brenda concentrated on her burger. She didn't say anything about Curtis Whitfield. *He probably won't call on me anyway.*

That evening Brenda got the shock of her life when Curtis knocked on the Branches's front door. Her brother answered.

"I'm Curtis Whitfield, and I'm here to see Brenda Lee."

"Why?"

"I reckon 'cause she told me to."

Brenda Lee heard the voices at the door and walked rapidly toward it, her gait awkward and her eyes straight ahead. She had changed into a pair of pedal pushers and a chambray shirt.

"Is that you Brenda Lee?"

"Hey Curtis."

"Can I come inside?"

"We can sit on the porch, but you'll have to sit on the steps."

Brenda sat in the teal and cream glider big enough for three people. Curtis sat and smoked on the front steps. Brenda's brother stood just inside the door, giving his mama and daddy the run down on what was happening out front.

Curtis did all of the talking. He told Brenda he had dropped out of school.

"I don't need no diploma," he said. "I'm an entrepreneur.

Brenda's heart swelled. She couldn't suppress her grin. *An ENTREPRENEUR! I knew Curtis had ambition and potential. I just knew it!* It didn't occur to Brenda that she should be surprised that a boy like Curtis would use a $64 word like that.

"What kind of business are you planning to operate?" she asked him.

"I don't want to be tied down by just one thing," Curtis told. "I want to see where the road takes me. You know, I've spent a lot of time around filling stations. I reckon I could open one of them, since a I know thing or two about cars. But I've spent a good bit of time around the drive-in, too. I wouldn't mind opening up little place somewhere away from Sumner. Shoot, I might even go into sales."

Curtis stood up, bowed toward Brenda, and delivered his sales pitch.

"Well, hello there ma'am. My name is Curtis Whitfield, and I was a-wonderin' if you had just 15 minutes to spare for me to tell you about the wonders of Fuller brushes and our extensive line of quality cleaning supplies?"

Brenda giggled. "You *are* a good salesman!"

"I just know I can't have a boss," Curtis said. "I can't be answering to nobody. I've been practically on my own my whole life. I ain't about to start answering to somebody now."

"Curtis, I bet you could be anything you set your mind to," Brenda said.

"Brenda! It's time to come in. The sun's almost gone!"

Brenda jumped to her feet. "I've got to go in, Curtis."

Leroy Branch's rule was that he said something to his kids only once.

"Brenda Lee, I was hoping we could go get that milkshake," Curtis said with a slight grin.

"Not today, Curtis. I've got to go."

Brenda went inside, the screen door slapping behind her.

Curtis whistled his way up the sidewalk towards the street.

"Who was that?" her daddy demanded, "and what does he mean showing up here this time of night."

The sky was far from dark. Brenda could still see the sun and read by its light, but if it was past 6, her daddy considered it night.

"That's Curtis Whitfield," Brenda told him. "He wanted to take me to get a milkshake."

"You ain't going to get no milkshake with a hoodlum," her daddy told her.

Curtis Whitfield was bad news. He had dropped out of school. He couldn't keep a job, and he bummed cigarettes, rides, gas and moonshine off everybody he met. Curtis smelled of stale tobacco, motor oil and sweat, and he was the first boy to give Brenda this kind of attention. Before the sun had set, Brenda was in love.

CHAPTER 7
LIFE IN SUMNER

For 90-some years, life in Sumner has revolved around the West Oaks cotton mill.

The mill opened back in the 1890s at the height of the second industrial revolution. The massive brick structure stands four-stories tall and takes up the whole west side of Maple Avenue. It spawned a mill village to the north and south of the mill itself, with block after block of white, two-story clapboard houses providing affordable shelter to the men and women who work at the mill, teach at the school and work in the few little stores that are in Sumner. Even now, in 1982, you still can set your watch by the West Oaks Mill whistle, signaling the end of one shift and the beginning of another at 7 a.m., 3 p.m. and 11 p.m.

A pair of railroad tracks still runs perpendicular to the mill's loading docks. frequented by the trains carrying bales of cotton to the mill and finished denim from it. Though a testament to commerce and important to mill operations, the railroad tracks became a source of frustration as the world grew more and more mobile. The trains often delayed parents trying to pick up their kids and teenagers trying to get to their after-school jobs in Paris. Sumner folks trying to get to or from work in Paris got bent out of shape by a train that took too long to do its job. When the train stopped, Sumner stopped. Cars backed up, bumper-to-bumper for half a mile. To this day the railroad tracks are the major cause of traffic jams in the little mill town, outside of football games and shift changes.

The buildings around the mill once housed businesses built to support the people who lived, worked and attended school in Sumner. There was a doctor's office, a pharmacy, the grocery store, the cafeteria, a laundromat, a high school, an elementary school and a couple of churches crowded in and around the mill village. And surrounding those buildings were baseball fields and practice fields where young athletes aspired to the big leagues.

Baseball was big in Sumner, bigger than football, stemming from a long history, dating back to the earliest mill days, but taking hold in the 1930s. When the Great Depression ushered in a need for people to find an inexpensive pastime, West Oaks formed a team made up of mill workers and a few star players from the high school. The West Oaks team played against teams from other textile mills in and around Sumner and Paris. Together, the mills formed their own baseball league. The local radio station broadcast the games. Some of the best players became baseball legends, none more legendary than Willie Nation, who went on to play professional ball. He even worked at the mill in the off season. Even after the mills quit sponsoring teams, baseball remained big. West Oaks High School was state champion in baseball several years running, and the whole town turned out for their games. School even let out early for big games against a championship rival.

Baseball is still big in Sumner, though the emphasis has shifted more to Little League. The training for the high school team starts early with four- and five-year-olds playing Tee Ball, eight-year-olds getting pitching lessons, and coaches demanding weekend practices. The teams take big-league names, and the uniforms mirror their professional counterparts. Of course, this is Georgia, so everybody has wanted to be a Brave ever since Atlanta got its team, but a Dodger or a Cub will do just fine. No one ever fields a Yankee team. This is, after all, the South.

In the fall, baseball gives way to football and cheerleading.

Like the spring baseball season, football Fridays bring out generations of Sumner residents to cheer on children, grandchildren neighbors, friends and children of friends. It might still be 90 degrees on a September night, but that doesn't matter. Crowds always fill the football stands at West Oaks High School, and when the weather finally cools, old letter jackets start filling the seats. Once a West Oaks letterman, always a West Oaks letterman. That's a fact not always welcomed by the coaches. With that many former players intently watching the game, every player has another 15 or 20 coaches in the stands barking orders, attempting to dictate plays and laboring through every down.

"Why are you holdin' the ball, T-bone? Pass it!"

"Block him. Block him, Sid. SID, BLOCK HIM! Good night, man! God gave you 300 pounds and big feet, USE 'EM!"

Cheering on the sidelines are girls from 5 to 18, jumping up and down with their gold and white pompoms. If their mamas could still wear their cheerleading uniforms, they'd be right there beside them. The cheerleaders pull their hair back into ponytails, made blonde from Sun-In, lemon juice or both, with enormous white bows wider than their heads. Their mamas watch from the stands with equally large and equally blonde hair, frosted, highlighted, tinted, permed, fried and sprayed into a glorious helmet of hot-rolled curls, teased and tucked into perfection.

In a town the size of Sumner, just about every student is either a cheerleader, football player or a member of the marching band. That's one reason why the home stand is always full. There are generally two or three generations of family members watching every move, whether the West Oaks Dragons were mighty or meek. Sumner is the kind of town where you can count on every booster club fundraiser being a success. The people there might not have much money, but they are always willing to share. If the cheerleaders have a car wash, there's a line of cars at the drive-in waiting. If the Pee Wees and Mites have a bake sale, every mama and grandmama bakes cookies or brownies, and every daddy buys them. The mill workers stuck together. That's what you did in Sumner.

At homecoming, everything gets bigger: The hair, the clothes, the crown and the crowds. Even the leaves on the trees seemed to get more colorful during homecoming week. The homecoming parade passes right in front of the mill, timed for shift-change, so that every mama and daddy can see their kids in the parade. Babies too young to go to school, last year's seniors, grandparents, neighbors and Sumner old timers line Maple Street when the marching Dragons key up their first song, and nobody leaves their spot on the road until the very last float has passed, even if that float was a kid on a bicycle. It's been that way since after the second World War, and nobody in town sees a reason to change it.

As homecoming fades into the past and the Thanksgiving turkey is reduced to bones and gristle, the lights of Christmas begin to shine. Every December the whole town becomes a little Bethlehem when mill workers pull a giant lighted star to shine between the mill's two towering smokestacks, casting a warm glow of grace high over Sumner. Like their love of baseball, the star is a holdover from the Depression when people needed a reminder that there was still a reason to hope. Since that time everybody who has lived, worked or gone to school or church in Sumner has taken notice of the Christmas star.

The pastor of First Baptist Church, which sits about as close to the star as the shepherds were to the manger, always includes the five-pointed star in the

Christmas Eve service. All the Baptists, which is more than half of Sumner, show up for the 5:30 p.m. service. It draws generations of people from all around, even Methodists, Presbyterians and the occasional Pentecostal. The preacher times the service so that the Sumner star is shining against the dark sky as people leave to go home and finish their preparations for Santa.

The pastor keeps the service simple. At 5:30 on the dot, the congregation sings *Oh Come All Ye Faithful*. He follows by reading from the second chapter of the gospel of Matthew to a dark and silent room, illuminated only by candles, their flames protected by clear-glass hurricane globes.

Now when Jesus was born in Bethlehem of Judaea in the days of Herod the king, behold, there came wise men from the east to Jerusalem, Saying, Where is he that is born King of the Jews? For we have seen his star in the east, and are come to worship him. When Herod the king had heard these things, he was troubled, and all Jerusalem with him. And when he had gathered all the chief priests and scribes of the people together, he demanded of them where Christ should be born. And they said unto him, In Bethlehem of Judaea: for thus it is written by the prophet, and thou

Bethlehem, in the land of Juda, art not the least among the princes of Juda: for out of thee shall come a Governor, that shall rule my people Israel. Then Herod, when he had privily called the wise men, enquired of them diligently what time the star appeared. And he sent them to Bethlehem, and said, Go and search diligently for the young child; and when ye have found him, bring me word again, that I may come and worship him also. When they had heard the king, they departed; and, lo, the star, which they saw in the east, went before them, till it came and stood over where the young child was. When they saw the star, they rejoiced with exceeding great joy. And when they were come into the house, they saw the young child with Mary his mother, and fell down, and worshipped him: and when they had opened their treasures, they presented unto him gifts; gold, and frankincense and myrrh.

After he finishes reading, three members of the congregation, an elementary-aged child, a parent or middle-aged adult, and a senior citizen, come to the pulpit and tell about their favorite Christmas memory.

Last year, nine-year-old Taylor had the church in stitches.

"When I was a kid," he started, "I used to think Christmas was about getting everything I wanted. Well, last year, I found out the hard way that that ain't always true."

The congregation snickered.

"I begged my mama for a new bicycle. I told Santa Claus I wanted a new bicycle, and I told my grandpaw I wanted a new bicycle.

"Well, come Christmas morning, I got up early and walked into the living room and right there was a bicycle. It was bright red and had racing handlebars. I ran over to it, jumped on it and knocked over the whole Christmas tree!"

The congregation burst into laughter, and Taylor grinned. He waited for the laughter to die down.

"I jumped off that bike as quick as I could and tried to stand the Christmas tree back up. Mama heard me and come a runnin' downstairs, and, well, I busted into tears.

"After I quit crying, me and mama started standing the Christmas tree back up, and she asked me what I was a doin.'

"I told her I was so excited about my new bicycle that I just couldn't help myself.

"That's when mama told me that the bicycle by the tree wasn't mine. It was for her. Santa left my bicycle was outside, 'cause he didn't want me to find it first thing.

"I got what I asked for, for Christmas, but I almost ruined it. All I was doing was thinking about myself. I didn't think about Santa brining mama a bicycle so she could ride with me. Mama said that's what happens when you make the presents more important than Jesus. After all, shouldn't we be giving *Him* presents? I mean, it's *His* birthday!"

The three perspectives are almost always heartwarming and almost always challenging, and by the end of the service, everybody has just a little bit better understanding of why Christmastime is so important in Sumner.

After a child speaks, a parent or middle-aged adult comes up and talks about hunting for peace in the middle of Christmas chaos or looking for ways to keep traditions alive. Then, an elderly speaker always brings the message home by focusing on family, enjoying their friends and family, or remembering a Christmas with a loved one who has passed on.

At the end of the service, everybody stands and sings *Silent Night,* as each person lights a candle from the person beside them. Then, still singing, everybody files out of the church and into the parking lot, carrying their own light. There, the pastor directs their attention to the big star suspended in the night sky. That's when he reminds everybody that the light in their hand is a light that draws others home to Jesus, just as the Sumner star draws friends and family members back home for the holidays, and just as that first Christmas star drew wisemen and shepherds to the stable. Then, with the kind of perfect timing that can only come from years of practice, just as the pastor finishes speaking, the church bell begins to ring, and Sumner knows that it is Christmas.

In between the seasons, the mill is hard, but honest work. The men and women who earn their wages there are proud, but that pride butts heads with the folks who live and work in Paris. The Paris-ites have tended to look down their noses at the West Oaks mill workers almost as long as the mill has been open, taking advantage of the easy and obvious name calling. After a long day at work in a mill swirling with fine blue cotton, just about every worker in the mill leaves with tiny balls of blue cotton stuck to their hair, their five-o'clock shadows, their shoelaces and whatever else the fiber could grab on to.

"They're all a bunch of lint heads," some jerk might say.

"His daddy is a lint head," you might hear somebody whisper.

Or, sometimes, it would be just a sneer, "Lint head." The words are usually filled with a pound of contempt and a few ounces of disgust, especially at rival ballgames or in parking lot disputes.

Though some tried to wear the invective like a badge of honor, using it to describe themselves, everyone in Sumner knows that it isn't. Still, when the people of Sumner gather in their little town, the pride of their history, what they've accomplished, and the value of their simple lives seems to sustain them in the face of the ugliness.

"There's no shame in hard work and an honest day's pay," somebody's granddaddy always said to a chorus of nods and replies.

"Nope."

"Sure ain't."

"No siree.

"No shame at all." The "at all" was always pronounced as one word, "a-tall," like "afoot" or "aloof," although it's doubtful anybody in Sumner had ever uttered the word "aloof."

The shared experience of life in the village fostered a sense of community that was hard to come by.

Sumner is the kind of place where you could count on seeing a friendly face at the pharmacy, get a helping hand at the hardware store or have a good conversation at the drive-in. It's the kind of place where you need to allow an extra hour for catching up after church, even if you've already seen each other at the grocery store, the football game or the beauty parlor.

It is the kind of town where, even if a boy or girl goes off to college, they are likely to come back home to put their education to use. A good many of West Oaks' teachers have been students there, the children and grandchildren of millworkers The same was true of store managers, preachers and just about anybody else who lives or works in Sumner, including the mill. Sumners take care of their own, and, for the most part, they are loyal to the death.

CHAPTER 8
FIRST KISS, 1956

Three generations of Branches had worked at the West Oaks mill, and the Monday morning after graduation, Brenda Lee Branch became the sixth member of her family to do so. Her granddaddy had worked at the mill, and her daddy and both her brothers still worked there. Even her mama had worked there for a while before she married her daddy. The mill had always kept a roof over their heads and food on their table. Her parents figured it would do the same for Brenda.

Like so many Sumner residents before her, it didn't take long for Brenda's life to take on the rhythms of the mill, but those first few days were difficult.

Turning bales of white cotton into blue denim is an industrial feat ill-suited for a girl who, like Brenda, had been sheltered from some of the more difficult truths of life. Cotton mills are loud and hot and filled with a fibrous haze. Mill workers are constantly in action, manning the whirring, spinning, shaking and shifting machines, each dependent on the humans who keep watch over them and feed their voracious appetites for more and more cotton. After unbaling, the ginned cotton is inspected then combed with metal bristles in the carding room. The carding process removes any hulls and dirt missed by the gins while straightening and untangling the fibers. These fibers are then moved to the spinning room where they become yarn. Some of the yarn is dyed the characteristic indigo blue, while some remains white. The yarn is then chemically reinforced before being wound on spools and eventually woven into denim cloth. Brenda was assigned to the spooling room.

 On her first day, she coughed and sneezed like she had been rolling in ragweed. It took a while, but Brenda eventually got used to the blue cotton that floated in the rare beams of sunlight and stuck to everything it came in contact with. She had never stood for that long, walked that much or heard that much noise in her whole life. Brenda's nerves were a mess, and she wasn't sure she'd make it to lunch. By the grace of God and the help of her trainer, she did. Before lunch time Brenda was covered head to toe in a layer of blue cotton lint, and by the end of the day, she guessed the lint had added 10 pounds to her weight.

After eight long hours of doing her part to turn cotton into denim, Brenda clocked out and walked to the parking lot to meet her brother, feeling heavier, a whole lot more tired, and a good bit accomplished. She wasn't a secretary or a teacher, but she was working, earning money and helping her family. These were good things.

The Branch house wasn't that far from the mill, but millwork was exhausting. If you could drive home instead of walk, it was the thing to do. Brenda and Robert rode to and from the mill with their daddy, giving her weary feet a brief, but welcomed reprieve before her house chores began.

When she got home, Brenda drug herself up the front porch steps and walked in the door of the mill house she shared with her mama, her daddy and her brother. She was sweaty, blue and bushed. She was thirsty, and she wanted a bath, but it was way too early for that. Plus, she had gotten home just in time to help mama with supper.

Brenda liked helping her mama, so much that once she got started, she forgot all about how tired she had been. She enjoyed the ritual of putting on one of mama's aprons, especially the pretty yellow one, and talking to her while they peeled potatoes or looked beans. Looking beans was something she had helped her mama do for as long as she could remember. Pintos in particular would often have a bad bean or a stone in them. The little rocks would wreak havoc on weak teeth. Brenda and her mama would talk about soap operas, relatives or church people, while they poured handfuls of beans on the table and slid them into a bowl a few at a time, removing the rocks as they went. Sometimes, they'd just listen to the radio. Most of the time the dial would be tuned to WZOT over in Honey Grove. They played the best gospel music. Mama liked The Chuckwagon Gang and The Blackwood Brothers. Brenda preferred The Florida Boys and the Kingsmen, but it was all good, four-part-harmony with a rumbling deep bass singer and a tenor who could sing so high you thought his voice probably reached the angels. They made you feel like Jesus was right there in the kitchen with you, at least that's what Brenda thought.

When Robert was at the house by himself, he would tune the kitchen radio to a country music station. Mama always said that was honkytonk music, but Robert didn't care, at least he didn't as long as mama was gone. Robert was usually pretty good about putting it back on mama's station, mainly because of how mad she'd get whenever he forgot.

"Souls in danger, look above,
"Jesus completely saves;

"He will lift you by his love
"Out of the angry waves."

Brenda washed her hands, and Mama slid a bowl of Irish (she called them "Arsh") potatoes across the chrome edged dinette set. Every Monday night for as long as she could remember supper was fried potatoes (everybody in the Branch house called them "taters") and chicken livers. Brenda's job was to peel and slice the taters while her mama fried the livers in the deep cast iron skillet. She tried singing along while she peeled.

"Love lifted me.
"Love lifted me.
"When nothing else would help.
"Love lifted me."

After supper, Brenda gathere.d the plates, glasses and bowls and started washing them, standing them in the dish drainer to let them air dry in the summer heat. She had one bowl left when Curtis Whitfield knocked on the door.

Brenda scurried to the door, drying her hands on the apron she was wearing.

"Hey Curtis," she said shyly.

"Brenda Lee Branch, can we go get that milk shake?"

Brenda glanced back toward her daddy who was glaring at the door.

"I can't Curtis."

"Well, can we sit on the porch again?"

"OK, but you still have to sit on the steps."

Curtis shook a cigarette out of the pack and sat on the second step from the top, leaning back on his elbow to look at Brenda, who was moving forward and back on the glider.

She thought she might tell him about her first day at the mill, but Curtis was too busy telling her about his day. He got to the filling station about noon. He watched the boys change the oil in Pete Hopper's Chevy and fill up a couple of radiators. After that, he went over to Stanley's to shoot the breeze and watch him bondo a banged-up Studebaker. According to Curtis, his friend planned to transform the clunker into a real hotrod to race.

"And ol' Stanley just happened to have a jar of moonshine out back," Curtis whispered, then laughed.

"Whoop!" Brenda exclaimed before she could catch herself. "You didn't drink none, did you Curtis?"

"Well, I had me a sip or two," he said.

She did not approve of moonshine drinking, but she reckoned she could forgive it if it was this one time.

It was clear that Curtis had lived more in the past 12 hours than Brenda had in the past two years.

"Ben was out there with us." He commenced to imitate stuttering Ben, who had difficulty spitting out a sentence but could service a transmission with his eyes closed and one hand tied behind his back.

"I, I, I, b-b-b-bet ya-ya-ya-y'all cuh-cuh-cuh can't t-t-t-tell me wh-wh-what I di-di-did to, to that car-car-carburetor."

Curtis laughed, but Brenda didn't. She'd been laughed at before, and she didn't appreciate people who laughed at somebody for something they couldn't help.

"That ain't nice, Curtis." "You ought not say things about people that they can't help."

Curtis changed his tune.

"Ol' Ben sure knows his way around a Chevy," Curtis said, watching Brenda to see if that would earn him a little redemption.

He didn't need it. Brenda's naïve optimism included a short memory. She always saw the best in people, even Curtis Whitfield.

I've got to go back in," Brenda said. "I've got to work in the morning."

Brenda stood, and Curtis, in one quick move, leapt from the step, slipped his arm around Brenda's waist, and kissed her squarely on the mouth.

Brenda caught her breath, rattled and exhilarated all at the same time.

"What's that in your hair?" Curtis asked, staring at a curl that just touched Brenda's neck.

"Look here," he said. Reaching up, he pulled a tiny, ball of indigo cotton out of Brenda's hair. "You're a lint head."

The words had barely escaped his mouth when Robert Branch's fist landed on Curtis's jaw.

"Git off my porch. I don't ever want to see your sorry face around here again."

Curtis stumbled back toward the steps while a horrified Brenda escaped through the door and into the house, running past her daddy's recliner to find sanctuary in the only place she could truly be alone: the house's tiny bathroom. The door slammed shut behind her. Brenda's face flushed, and tears welled in her eyes than rolled down her ruddy cheeks. She splashed water on her face, grabbed a towel to dry her face and her tears, then caught a glimpse of her reflection in the mirror for the first time since she had gotten home. She saw what Curtis had seen. Caught in the Aqua Net shield that had held her hair somewhat in place were tiny balls of blue lint from the mill.

The tears returned. Curtis Whitfield was right. She was a lint head. *But he didn't have to say it!*

The radio in the kitchen was playing an old hymn.

"Are we weak and heavy-laden,
Cumbered with a load of care?
Precious Savior, still our refuge—
Take it to the Lord in prayer;
Do thy friends despise, forsake thee?
Take it to the Lord in prayer;
In His arms He'll take and shield thee,
Thou wilt find a solace there."

That was the last time Brenda Lee Branch saw Curtis Whitfield.

He was her first love and her first kiss, and she would never forget him.

CHAPTER 9
IT HAPPENED AT THE WORLD'S FAIR

Brenda didn't know much about the 1982 World's Fair other than it was in Knoxville. Tennessee, but if it was anything like the one Elvis Presley had gone to, well, it was a place worth seeing.

Twenty years earlier, Seattle, Washington hosted the World's Fair, and Elvis Presley filmed a movie about it. If the Knoxville version even resembled the movie, then a World's Fair might just be the most romantic place on earth. Elvis's fair was gleaming white and modern. There were space-age buildings, a Jetson's tower with a needle that stretched to the sky and a train that ran on one rail, way above the ground, that traffic never had to stop for. She could still remember Elvis's sly grin when he picked up his guitar and started singing *One Broken Heart for Sale* as he walked through the trailer court.

Based on what she remembered from Elvis's movie, the World's Fair would be nothing like the Eubanks County Fair. Every fall, the county fair set up shop at the fairgrounds over in Paris. Everybody went to it at some point during the week. The midway boasted a double Ferris wheel, a merry-go-round, a fun house and Brenda's favorite, *The Scrambler*—a shiny silver ride that would sling you back and forth in your seat as it spun circles within a circle. It was best to ride *The Scrambler* with three people in the seat. The force of the ride would sling two people to and fro. Riding with just one person in the seat meant you were asking for crick in your neck for sure.

Back in the day, the county fair had a show where a man turned into a gorilla right before your very eyes. It was way scarier than the haunted house ride, which wasn't much more than an excuse for teenagers to neck in the dark. There was one little hill inside the house that gave Brenda a bit of a fright, but the rest of it was just darkness and the occasional wolf howl. Leroy and Robert would go see the hoochie-coochie show after mama died. Brenda didn't know what kind of business went on in there, but she knew from the outside that it involved women with way too much skin showing and flirty music. She was pretty sure Jesus wouldn't approve.

A few steps from the midway, were two big metal structures. One housed 4-H projects and art done by kids from all the schools. In the other, women from five counties competed against each other in homemaking and crafting. Brenda always liked to see who won the blue ribbons, even though she thought it kind of funny that the people who came to see the exhibit didn't get to taste the canning entries.

"I mean, it's one thing to put up a jar of tomatoes or strawberry preserves that looks real nice, but it don't matter how good they look if they don't taste good," Brenda always said.

Women from all over brought their best jams, prettiest quilts, tightest crocheted afghans, biggest roses, most complicated needlepoint pillows and framed elaborate cross-stitch projects to be displayed for a week and judged by Margie Roebuck, the county's main home economist. Margie enlisted the help of a group of homemaking club presidents from outside the valley to help her judge. She didn't trust the local girls to be unbiased in their judging.

Brenda never entered anything in the fair. She had learned to can vegetables and make jellies and jams from her mama, but she had always heard that Margie was a tough judge. Everything had to be perfect, including the labels, or Margie wouldn't give a jar any points. Brenda didn't have time to be worrying about how pretty a jar of canned tomatoes was. She just needed to make sure she had plenty for the winter when you couldn't buy a decent tomato at the store.

The Eubanks County Fair also included a livestock barn that smelled like hay and cow manure. It was filled with pigs, cows, goats, lambs, and usually there was an egg incubator where chickens would hatch right before your very eyes. 4H-ers showed the animals they had raised from birth. The livestock was judged on their weight, their health and their disposition. Brenda always liked looking at the big-eyed cows. Most of them looked friendly, but every once in a while, Brenda would see one that just seemed sad. Brenda had a habit of stopping to talk to the sad cows.

"Hey there, girl. You missin' home?" She would look at them straight in the eye. "I see them big ol' eyes. I know you're sad. I wish I had an apple for you. You want some of this hay?"

Sooner or later, Brenda would flinch, jump back and hurry to the baby chicks.

"I tell you," she said out loud to herself, "that cow can see into my soul."

Her favorite part of the fair, though, was the food. She never ate supper on the day she went to the fair, so she'd have plenty of room for a corn dog and a roasted ear of corn. And she always made sure to have enough money to come home with a bag of pink and blue cotton candy.

For one week every summer, the fair lit up the Paris night sky like what Brenda imagined Las Vegas must be like. The carnies barked at the teenage boys, taunting them to prove their manhood by tossing rings around the necks of bottles, shooting down tin targets or knocking over a stack of milk bottles with a baseball. The boys who were good at it won giant blue stuffed dogs that had to be 3-foot tall. They promptly gave them to their girlfriends to hold onto the rest of the night. It was the same kind of ritual as a girl wearing a boy's class ring or letter jacket. If a girl was carrying a big stuffed dog, she had her a boyfriend and a date for the next weekend. Guaranteed.

Back in high school, Brenda had always wished a boy would win her one of the giant blue dogs like other girls had, but that never happened. Still, she was genuinely happy for the girls who did get one, and she showed it by smiling and speaking to every one of them as they passed by her on the midway.

"Oh! You got you one of them big dogs!" she would say to a perfect stranger.

"Whoop! Would you look at that? That dog is as big as you are!" she would call out as a teenager passed.

Brenda imagined there wouldn't be any blue ribbons for jelly or prophesying cows at the Knoxville World's Fair. No sir, a World's Fair would be fancy and sophisticated, like the Elvis movie. She envisioned a monorail, the smiling faces of people from all over the world and a busy midway so clean you could eat anything you dropped on it.

It would be beautiful and exciting. Poor Elvis might have been dead, but Johnny Cash and Ronald Reagan were gonna be in Knoxville. Tennessee didn't have a Space Needle, but it did have the Sun Sphere. Brenda had seen it on television. It was a shiny gold disco ball sitting on top of a tower, and it looked out over the fairgrounds. She didn't know what it did, but she hoped you could go up inside it. The tv promised rides and exhibits from a bunch of overseas countries. It was as close as Brenda was ever going to get to seeing what the rest of the world looked like. She wanted to go.

It wasn't that she didn't like Sumner. She did, but Brenda couldn't help the yearning in her heart for something special in her life. Going to the beauty shop, eating Jordan almonds at a wedding reception every now and then, working at the mill and eating chicken and dumplings every Thursday night had made her world small.

I feel like you, she thought one day in Paris when she stopped outside the pet store window. She was watching a little brown hamster in a cage, running furiously on its circular treadmill. *You have the necessities of life, but, poor thang, you're runnin' hard and getting' nowhere.* Brenda never wanted a hamster, or anything else that had to be confined, for that very reason. It just didn't seem right to keep an animal in a cage like that.

Brenda wasn't the kind of person to hate her life or anybody else's. She didn't. She was grateful to the Lord for her blessings, but she couldn't help but wonder about what could have been. She figured the World's Fair was the kind of place where anything could happen. It's where she could leave her mill life behind for a few days and maybe, just maybe find true love.

CHAPTER 10
SUITCASE PACKED

"I'll see you at church tomorrow," Miss Edna said as Brenda started up the walkway.

Brenda involuntarily widened her eyes. *Oh Lordy, what should I say? I can't lie to Miss Edna, especially about church!*

We'll see!" Brenda said, overcompensating her conundrum with her inflection.

With not a single trace of blue cotton in her hair, Brenda turned and waved, then waited until Miss Edna's car turned the corner on to Avenue D. Just as she had hoped for, Brenda's daddy and brother were gone, *Lord knows where.* She hurried into the house, went straight to her bedroom and slid a frost blue suitcase from underneath her old iron bed.

The suitcase had been used in the Branch family for years, primarily as the hospital suitcase. When her mama had been in the hospital, the blue suitcase with the elastic pocket on the inside of the lid, carried her extra panties, house shoes, gowns and a change of clothes to go home in. When Leroy had been in the hospital for a dizzy spell a few years ago, the blue suitcase accompanied him. The same blue suitcase had gone to Eubanks County Hospital twice with Brenda.

Brenda's hospital visits were only talked about in whispers. She had always had a problem with her nerves, at least that's the way her mama put it, and both hospitalizations were related to her condition. There had been an incident 17 years earlier when Brenda's nerves got the best of her, sending her to Eubanks County's psychiatric unit for a few days. The suitcase had gone with her, although she wasn't the one who packed it. More recently, the blue luggage also had accompanied her when she went in for her hysterectomy.

Brenda's doctor, aware of her excitability and anxiety, had prescribed the removal of her ovaries and uterus as a fix for her nervous condition. Brenda had never been married, wasn't likely to ever want to bear children, and she had already passed 40. He scheduled the surgery before Brenda or her daddy even had time to think about it. If the surgery was supposed to help Brenda's nerves, the sudden interruption of hormone production did the opposite. And, as the only woman in a house of men, she had no one to talk to about it.

So, she took every opportunity to bring it up, not always at the most opportune times.

"You know I had *female surgery*," Brenda once said to a young girl operating the grocery store cash register, whispering the last two words of her statement.

"Brenda," Miss Edna interrupted, "I'm sure she doesn't have time to talk about such personal things right now."

The cashier glanced at Miss Edna with a sense of relief before continuing ringing up the groceries.

She had a habit of mentioning her female surgery at the wedding receptions she and Rogene crashed on the weekends too.

"Why, hey, Mizz Burkhalter! I don't think I've seen you since I had my *female surgery*," Rogene overheard Brenda saying at one wedding.

"Girl, come over here and get a sip of this punch! You don't need to be talking about your surgery on such a happy day!" Rogene said, taking Brenda's elbow and steering her toward the punch bowl.

Everything she needed was in the suitcase. Brenda had packed her lupus medicine and her sugar tablets, which helped regulate her insulin. Her favorite dresses, including the yellow one from last Easter, were in there along with a pair of white pumps that she had only worn three times. She also had packed six pairs of pastel-colored cotton panties and three white brassieres, her two newest night gowns, a house coat and her Isotoners. In the side pocket, she had a toothbrush and toothpaste, some Shower-to-Shower powder and an unopened bottle of Avon Soft Musk that she would use sparingly. And laying right on top, was a folded map showing the Southeastern United States.

Brenda Lee was going to the World's Fair. She had found the map in the glove compartment of Robert's car and traced the route to Knoxville with her finger. She knew she would need to head toward Jasper, and just in case she got lost or forgot the way, she had made sure to tuck the map safely in her suitcase.

Wearing her favorite pink polyester pants and rose-print blouse, Brenda took her pocketbook and her suitcase and walked out the door. Inspired by Jane Ellen's fearlessness and kicking Paul Harvey's 100-year-old's advice to the curb, Brenda Lee Branch started walking purposefully north toward Tennessee.

Brenda had cashed her paycheck on Friday and specifically asked for most of it to be in ones, fives and tens. The Branches didn't bother with checking accounts. Every Friday, after they got paid, the first stop was First National Bank in Paris. Most of the mill workers walked over to McHenry's grocery store, right across from the mill. The store made a point to keep enough cash on Fridays to cash paychecks. Starting at about 3:10 p.m., McHenry's could count on a line of mill workers forming at the cash register, signed checks in hand. For as long as she could remember, even before her daddy retired from the mill, the Branches had bypassed the line at McHenry's and driven the six miles to Paris to cash their checks. Brenda never thought to ask why. Since she was dependent on her daddy and her brother for transportation, she just followed their lead.

Brenda had folded up three 20s and put them in her top dresser drawer. She'd left that money there for her daddy in case he needed grocery money or help with the bills while she was gone. The rest of her check, exactly $111.20, she put in her pocketbook—figuring she'd need a hotel room. She also planned on offering some gas money to whoever drove her to Knoxville. Plus, she'd need to eat at a restaurant or buy something to snack on at a filling station on the way. She figured $111 ought to do it. After buying a two-day ticket to the World's Fair for $15.95, she hoped she'd have enough left to buy some souvenirs and pay somebody to give her a lift back home.

Brenda's original plan had been to get Miss Edna or Rogene to drive her to the bus station so that she could take a Greyhound to Knoxville. But two things got in the way of that idea. First, Miss Edna and Rogene would want to know why she was going to the bus station. They wouldn't understand. So, she decided she'd best keep the details to herself. Second, when she called the Greyhound station, she got the shock of her life. They wanted $17 for a one-way ticket to

Knoxville. ONE WAY! That was half a day's wages! The ticket to the fair was outlandish enough. No sir, she'd walk a-ways and catch a ride with somebody.

It wasn't a great plan, but it would have to do.

CHAPTER 11
GATLINBURG, TENNESSEE, 1982

Curtis Whitfield had spent his whole life avoiding work. He hustled drunks at pool halls, bummed cigarettes from teenagers, talked up waitresses at every Dairy King and drive-in he could find, getting by on cons and lies. Every once in a while, he'd get a job at a filling station or garage, but those only lasted until they realized Curtis was helping himself to the merchandise and spending more time looking busy than actually doing the work.

After leaving Sumner, he wandered from Peachtree City to Johnson City, surviving on theft and charm. Along the way, he married and divorced four times. Well, *he* didn't divorce anybody. His ex-wives divorced him, usually for abandonment long after he had skipped town and moved on. He didn't know if he had any kids and didn't care. For 26 years he had managed to avoid Vietnam, extended work and the law. He had no intention of taking on responsibility now. To Curtis Whitfield's way of thinking, life was about as good as a man could ask for.

    Curtis had hitched his way to Maryville, but his opportunities for hustling were limited there since the college wasn't in session. So, he made his way 40 or so miles east to Gatlinburg. He was staying in a Knights Inn outside of town, spending his days people watching, stealing, pawning and charming. People dropped dollars in the Smokies like gamblers did in Las Vegas, and Curtis was betting on his chances to get ahold of some of that money. Gatlinburg and Cherokee, North Carolina were money magnets to be sure. Every little log cabin shop had some kind of Great Smoky Mountains trinket, Cherokee Indian knock off or air-brushed T-shirt for sale. Tourists were willing to pay to see everything from Guinness world record holders to a black bear in a cage or a chance to ride a roller coaster at Silver Dollar City. A guy like Curtis could blend in with the crowd, share a smoke and eat a good meal just by jawing with the right teenager, talking up a good Christian family or smiling at the right lady. Somehow or another he ended up with the $14.99 a night he needed to fall asleep on a purple crushed velvet bedspread to get rested up for the next day's hustle.

The hustles centered on a central theme around which Curtis had developed five stories. He'd watch somebody, stand nearby to hear their conversation, the sidle up to them for the con. More often than not, his efforts focused on women and teen-agers.

"Hey, uh, I hope you don't think I'm buttin' in, but I just heard y'all say y'all was from Georgia. I don't reckon you've spent any time around Peachtree City, have you?"

The art of a good lie was to start with the truth. He'd spent enough time in Peachtree City or several other places that he could talk about them with confidence, gaining the trust of his target.

Curtis would flash a smile and work his magic.

"I used to work in Peachtree City, down at the Texaco, with Bert Bridges. Do y'all know Bert? Well, anyways, I got offered a job with Delta, and I thought that was the place to be. They sent us up here to Gatlinburg for training. They wanted us to be able to tell passengers and such about the touristy things you can do around here."

Curtis drug his story out a while longer, hit the runway and finally landed his plane.

"So, here I stand. A sick mama back in Georgia, a plane ticket to Atlanta, and not a dime to my name to get me to the Knoxville airport."

After a couple of similar conversations, Curtis had $40 and the phone number of a nurse who worked at Grady Hospital down in Atlanta.

The idea of heading to Knoxville came when Curtis was standing outside the Ripley's Believe It or Not! museum in Gatlinburg one afternoon. He overheard a blonde with big, stiff hair talking about the World's Fair and was instantly intrigued.

He didn't know what a World's Fair was, but if people were willing to pay $16 just to get in for a couple of days, it sounded like the kind of place he needed to check out. He had made some easy money doing a little carnie work at a few county fairs. The admission price to most of them was $2 or $3. This must be some more fair if they were charging that kind of price to get in.

The big-haired woman seemed to be with a group of people. The fact that all but one had blonde hair and freckles suggested they were in the same family. Curtis did the math in his head. If they all planned on going, they'd shell out nearly $100 just to get through the gate to the fair. If they had that kind of money to throw away, Curtis figured they, and other rich people like them, had money for him. Even if the fair wasn't full of blue bloods, he was sure it had potential.

Blondie had said this was the *World's Fair.* Curtis could already see himself with a beer-drinking German girl or maybe a Japanese cutie. He smiled a broad smile. Curtis was going to Knoxville.

He caught a ride to a truck stop near the interstate and hopped an 18-wheeler headed to Knoxville. When the transfer truck he was riding in approached on I-40, Curtis's eyes caught sight of the big gold ball that welcomed the world to east Tennessee. It wasn't as impressive as the Atlanta skyline, but it was eye-catching enough. After the trucker let him out, Curtis used the World's Fair's golden orb as a landmark and landed at a Red Roof Inn for the night. He had a little over $22 in his pocket after he paid for his room. That would get him a pack of smokes, a couple cups of coffee and a meal or two in his belly before he figured out a way to get into the fair without buying a ticket.

Sure enough, Curtis hustled his way right in the next day, telling the gatekeeper he was there for a job interview. He spent the next month or so talking up college girls young enough to be his daughters and tired fair workers old enough to be his mama.

"Did I hear you say you was going to college?" he said to one of the girls. "I wanted to go back when I was younger, but Vietnam liked to have killed me.

"I don't talk much about it, you know? They's just some things you can't forget after you see them," Curtis would say, looking down as if he was in pain and without a trace of shame in his voice.

The typical young woman would have a look of horror on her face, afraid Curtis might be about to tell her more than she wanted to know. He had this conversation down to a science.

"Looky here, you don't want to know 'bout that stuff. Where can a veteran get beer around here? Uh, I didn't catch your name."

After learning her name, Curtis would hook his prey as easy as if he was fishing for catfish in a muddy river.

Drawing the young woman's name out longer than it was ever intended to be, Curtis would drop his chin, then look up at her with a sly smile and ask, "Did you say you knew where I could get a beer?"

That's all it took for Curtis to get a lead on a kid named Todd who could hook him up with free beer.

Curtis Whitfield had scored again.

Within ten minutes he had ambled over to the Biergarten, found Todd and was sipping on a cold one.

Before their conversation was over, Curtis had secured a connection to an endless supply of free beer and a place to sleep if he needed it. Most days he walked away from the fair with a full belly, a beer buzz and a place to sleep to boot.

Within a week, Curtis had figured out all the places he could while away the hottest part of the day, the food vendors where he could get a free meal, the kids who would give him a cigarette when he ran out and the best places to meet families who would buy his story. In his estimation, life was going good for Curtis Whitfield.

If it wasn't one of the fair girls that reminded him of naïve Brenda Lee Branch, maybe it was the German beer or the monotony of fair life day after day. Whatever the trigger, the memory of the Sumner lint heads and a kiss on a porch that led to sore jaw soon had Curtis tired of the fair, the cheap hotels and the Tennessee tourists. He needed a new wife and a new life, somewhere slower, somewhere quieter, somewhere like Sumner, where he wouldn't have to work so hard at not working.

CHAPTER 12
INVITATION TO KNOXVILLE

The phone had rung just as Brenda was cleaning up the supper dishes. Brenda wiped her hands on a dish towel and grabbed the receiver from its cradle.

"Hello?"

"Brenda Lee?" Curtis had hatched his plan while drinking one of Todd's free beers. He bummed a few quarters "to call his sick mama" and dialed Brenda Lee Branch's number, betting it would be the same.

"Who is this?" Brenda didn't have time for nonsense. She had jumped right into cooking supper as soon as she got in the house from her shift at the mill. Now, her brother and daddy had their legs propped up in the living room while she stood at the sink washing the melamine dishes in water as hot as they could stand it. Her mama had taught her that dishes weren't clean unless they were washed in the hottest water possible. She was sweating. Her hands were red and burning. Her feet were sore. Her legs were tired. All she wanted was to sit down and watch a little TV.

"Who is this, again?"

"Brenda Lee, it's Curtis Whitfield. Brenda Lee? Brenda Lee?"

"Hello?" The man's voice said again.

"Did you say this was Curtis Whitfield? From Sumner? *That* Curtis Whitfield?"

Curtis laughed. *It is Curtis. Heaven help me!* Brenda could picture his grin through the phone line.

"Curtis, you know I can't talk to you."

Flustered, she could feel her face burning. She was sure it had turned red. She had started to pace. *Why was Curtis Whitfield calling?* She hadn't talked to a boy, uh, man, she'd been interested in like *that* since, well, since she'd last talked to Curtis. She knew she needed to keep her voice down, but she couldn't help herself. Whenever she got excited, Brenda's voice rose with her degree of excitement. She had to concentrate to keep herself in check. *Keep calm, Brenda Lee. It's just Curtis Whitfield.*

"You mean to tell me after 26 years you still can't make your own decisions about who you talk to?" Curtis asked. "Look here. I'm in Knoxville at the World's Fair. I'm gonna be here the rest of this month, and since Sumner ain't but a few hours away, I thought it sure would be nice to find out how you was a doin'."

Brenda was beside herself. She suddenly felt 18 again. She unconsciously lifted her left hand to touch her brown helmet of hair, which still bore traces of blue lint, just like the lint Curtis had called out those many years ago. It was an involuntary movement, like touching a scar from a long-ago injury. She had come to reckon with this side effect of millwork. A lifetime in the cotton mill meant the blue lint was likely to always be there.

"You're at the World's Fair!" Brenda exclaimed, too loud.

"Hey! What's all the commotion? The Braves is on!" her daddy shouted from the living room. She had failed to keep her voice in check. Brenda caught herself, then continued. "I can't even imagine! I've seen commercials about it on TV! I'd love to see something like that in person!"

Curtis had his opening.

"Well, look here now, the way I see it, you owe me a milkshake date. Why don't you come up here and let me show you around? Brenda Lee, they've got sites like you've never seen before. Part of the Great Wall of China is right here. Dinah Shore and Ronald Reagan came up here to see everything. It's a wonder to behold!"

For the next several minutes, Curtis deposited conned quarters into the payphone so he could tell Brenda about the exotic things he'd seen in Knoxville, the gold Sun Sphere, the giant Rubik's Cube and the building that looked like China had landed in the Great Smokey Mountains. The $1.50 he spent on that phone call was an investment in his future.

"China!" Brenda said. "Why, I just … I can't even imagine!"

"Brenda Lee, darlin,' I've got to get back to work. You think about it, okay? Can I call you tomorrow?"

"Work!" Brenda's voice was an octave higher and several decibels louder. *Curtis Whitfield had a job! He had to get to work!* "I have to work too, but you can call me after. I get home about 3:30."

And there it was. Before long, if Curtis Whitfield's plans worked out, he would be headed back to Sumner, where Brenda and her steady paycheck awaited. But first, he needed to get Brenda Lee to Knoxville.

Curtis had called Brenda every day for the next five days. He told her about the Australian windmills, King Tut's tomb, and the German food he tried. Sensing that she needed a little extra convincing, Curtis used one of his five stories to bait Brenda into believing that he needed saving and only she could do it.

"Brenda Lee, I'm afraid I've made a mess of my life," he told her.

Brenda steeled herself. *I was afraid of that.* She knew Curtis had seen trouble, but after more than 20 years had passed, she hoped he had risen above it.

"I've been married four times," Curtis said with all the sadness he could muster.

FOUR TIMES! Brenda stopped herself from saying it out loud. She had never in her life known anybody who had been married more than twice, outside of Elizabeth Taylor, and she didn't really count 'cause she really didn't know her anyway.

"Curtis? That's an *awful* lot of marriages," Brenda said quietly, emphasizing the word "awful."

"Like I said, I've made a mess of things. Look here, they was all good women, they was. I mean, the first girl, we was just too young to get married. I couldn't blame her when she said she wanted to marry the boy who took her to her senior prom. I was too busy working and not spending enough time with her."

"She left you?" *Well, that wasn't Curtis's fault.*

"Yea, but I'm tellin' you, I can't blame her. My second marriage came about after I met this girl at church."

He met a girl at church! Brenda *knew* he had turned his life around.

"What happened to her, Curtis?"

"Well, I found out real quick that just 'cause a woman goes to church don't mean she lives for the Lord."

Hallelujah! Curtis Whitfield was talking about Jesus!

"Don't get me wrong," Curtis continued. "She wasn't a bad person. It's just that she had a drinking problem that she just couldn't turn over to Him, you know? Brenda, you know I've done some drinking in my past, but I just couldn't live with a gal who claimed she had quit drinking, but really hadn't."

"Bless your heart, Curtis! No, you couldn't!" Brenda didn't doubt a single word he told her.

"The end of my third marriage was completely on me," Curtis told her. "I had gotten this job that took me out of town more than it should have. She just got lonely. I came home after a two-week road trip up north, working for Delta, to find a note that she loved me, but that she was leaving me."

Daddy and Robert had been wrong! Curtis was a hard worker. He worked for Delta airlines. Brenda didn't know anybody who worked for an airplane company!

"Oh Curtis! Here you was trying to make a good livin' for somebody, working for a big company, and she just wrote you a Dear John letter? You're breaking my heart!"

Number four, he told her, was a girl he thought he could trust, but found out he couldn't.

"I don't want to go into the details. They'd embarrass me and you. But here's the thing Brenda Lee, I think I've 'bout got it figured out. The reason didn't none of these marriages work out is because of one thing: None of them women could hold a candle to you."

Brenda's face could not have burned any hotter. Tears were stinging her eyes. Here she was, 44 years old, and for the first time in her life, a man had told her she was special.

"I ain't never forgot our kiss on your front porch, Brenda Lee. Do y'all still live there in the mill village?"

Brenda told him she did and that not a lot had changed in Sumner since he'd been gone.

"I still live with Robert and daddy. Mama died years ago. I've been working at the mill ever since I graduated. I go to the beauty shop on Saturdays, and, of course, we have church every Sunday."

Curtis wasn't listening. He had a plan to execute.

"Come to Knoxville," Curtis interrupted, as if that was a brand-new idea that had just popped into his mind. "This place shuts down at the end of October. There will never be another chance for you to see this much of the world in one place. Come to Knoxville. Let me show you what Korea looks like."

Brenda's mind had begun to race. *Could I actually go to the World's Fair? Could Curtis and I actually spend some time together, like on a date? Reckon we could finally have that milkshake?* Maybe she could go to for a weekend. She'd make sure to set aside some money in case her daddy needed something for him or Robert. Her weekly trip to the beauty shop only cost $7 unless she was getting her four-times a year permanent wave, but she could get by without new curls until August. She'd have to finish out the workweek, but if she counted her pennies, she just might have enough money for a bus ticket and a hotel room for two nights. Her heart was beating out of her chest.

Back in the kitchen, mama's radio played.

"I'll go with him through the garden,
I'll go with him through the garden,
I'll go with him through the garden,
I'll go with him, with him all the way

Where he leads me, I will follow,
Where he leads me, I will follow,
Where he leads me, I will follow,
I'll go with him, with him all the way."

CHAPTER 13
A TRIP UP HIGHWAY 53

When Brenda called the Greyhound station that next day to ask about tickets, she nearly lost her breath when they told her how much it'd be to ride from Paris to Knoxville.

"SEVENTEEN DOLLARS!" Her voice shrilled. *It's a good thing I'm here by myself.*

She would *not* pay the outlandish price of $17 to ride *one-way* on a bus full of strangers, round-trip maybe, but *one way*? No ma'am! The cost of gas had gone up, but Greyhound wasn't no limousine! She would just have to catch a ride. Giddy excitement pushed aside the fear that normally would have accompanied that kind of idea. In just a few days, she would be having that long-awaited milkshake with Curtis Whitfield.

She had thought about him often over the years, whenever she would go to a wedding with Rogene or see a couple holding hands at the grocery store. When she saw *West Side Story,* she was Maria, and Curtis was Tony. People didn't want them to be together. She sure was glad Curtis hadn't ended up like Tony. That would be too much to bear.

The rest of that week felt like waiting for Christmas after you had bought and wrapped all the gifts and all that was left was opening them. Curtis called her twice more to make sure she was coming, and Brenda told him not to worry.

"I've got my suitcase packed, some extra money in my wallet, and I'm getting my hair done before I leave on Saturday," Brenda told him.

Brenda had secretly packed her suitcase and stored it under her bed, the only real estate she claimed as her own, even though she wasn't sure that it was really hers. She had slept in that old iron bed that belonged to her grandmother and then her mother, for as long as she could remember. It had once been white, with a thicker outer frame. Within the frame were thin iron bars running horizontally and vertically. At each intersection was a cast iron fleur-de-lis. Brenda and her mama just called them irises. Brenda had inherited her mama's apron and her housekeeping duties, but she wasn't too sure her daddy and Robert counted the bed as her property.

She had gone to work every day, unable to hide her smile. She could sense that people were looking at her funny, but she couldn't help it. *Get ahold of yourself, Brenda. It wouldn't never do for daddy, Robert or Miss Edna to find out what you're planning.* Her daddy and her brother noticed that her behavior had changed, but they figured she was just having female trouble or that her nervous condition was flaring up. So, they ignored it. Thankfully, nobody said anything, because Brenda didn't think she'd be able to keep her secret if they did. Every evening after supper, she would go to her room, pull the suitcase from under her bed and re-check her packing list, making sure she had everything she needed, always wondering whether Curtis would like her choices.

When Saturday came, it took every ounce of strength that Brenda could muster not to tell Miss Edna and the girls what she was planning. She was practically jumping in her seat she was so excited.

She planned to be in Knoxville by evening. It was an 8-hour bus ride, counting all the stops in between. She figured if she left Paris no later than 11, she'd be in Knoxville by 7 with any luck at all.

Tally, Teresa and Miss Edna all noticed that Brenda was noticeably more excitable at the shop, but Brenda had had spells like that before, so, like her family, they tried to ignore her.

"Did y'all know The World's Fair was in Knoxville?" Brenda said too loudly and to no one in particular.

"I've heard about it," Tally said, "but I don't reckon I've got no business going up there where all them people are. I'd rather go to the beach."

"I think I might like to see it," Brenda said. "You could probably get there in a day, don't you think?"

"Well, you could drive there in probably 4 or 5 hours," Teresa said, "and you'd be right there at Cherokee, Gatlinburg and Pigeon Forge."

"I read you could buy a six-month pass for $100," Brenda said. "Can you imagine?"

"Why would anybody in their right mind what to go to a fair for six months?" Miss Edna asked rhetorically. "No thank you. One night at the Eubanks County Fair is about all I can handle."

"I bet the World's Fair is different," Brenda said. "There ain't no telling who you'll meet at The World's Fair."

"Like Elvis Presley, if he was still alive," Teresa said. "I'd go there to see Elvis."

The women in the shop laughed and nodded. Elvis had been gone for a few years, but no one had yet replaced him in their hearts.

With their hair freshly washed and styled, Brenda and Miss Edna drove back to the mill village. Paul Harvey had been on, but Brenda didn't hear a word he said. After assuring Miss Edna that she did not need to go to the grocery store, Brenda walked slowly and deliberately through the gate and up the sidewalk towards the old screen door. She had been careful not to say she'd see Miss Edna at church on Sunday. She didn't want to tell a lie to her dear friend, and she didn't want someone so wise to give her any more doubts than she already had.

Miss Edna's Buick hadn't made it more than a couple of blocks down Avenue D when Brenda, suitcase in hand, walked out the door. She made quick work of the sidewalk and headed up the street toward

Maple Avenue. She would not hitchhike in Sumner. It was the safest place to catch a ride into town, but people would talk. She had called Rogene to see if she could give her a ride, but Rogene said she was busy. She couldn't ask Robert or her daddy. They would ask too many questions, so Brenda had decided she would walk the six miles to Paris and find somebody there who was headin' north and willing to drive her as far as they would or could.

Brenda walked quickly and purposefully, like she had forgotten something at the store or had an important meeting to go to like the women on TV, their heels clicking on the tile floors. *But I'm not headed to the store, and I ain't never been to an important meeting in my life. No ma'am. I'm going to meet my boyfriend.*

"Whoop!" she said out loud. She had never called Curtis her boyfriend before.

It took Brenda a good 20 minutes to get to the rock bridge in front of the mill. She crossed the railroad tracks at First Baptist Church and walked up the hill toward the Methodist church. The incline took her breath a little. So, she slowed down a bit, but she made it, and thankfully, the road leveled out. She continued on Maple, walking past the identical white clapboard two-story houses that still largely sheltered millworkers. She hoped she wouldn't see anybody she knew. She didn't want to have to explain why she had a suitcase with her headed toward Paris.

    Brenda had never walked all the way to the funeral home before, but here she was, and honestly, she wasn't even tired. The adrenaline in her system and her heart full of Curtis fueled her on. She felt her face. It must have been flushed from the lupus and the heat, but *I'm doing alright. No, I'm doing better than alright.* The mill houses had become brick ranchers, and the traffic picked up some, but Brenda kept on walking. She followed Maple for another hour, reaching its end at the old depot where a passenger train used to stop to take shoppers to Rich's in Atlanta. *It sure would be nice if there was a train to Knoxville.* She wondered if a train ride might have cost less than a bus ticket, but she couldn't think about that now. She needed to get to Highway 53. That meant crossing the bridge over the Etowah and heading up the hill to the old Kroger store, where her mama had redeemed her S&H Green Stamps for a toaster one time. *I used to love puttin' them stamps in books for Mama. Mama, if you can hear me, I hope you ain't mad for me going to meet Curtis. I think I love him.*

It was evening before Brenda made it to the White Columns Funeral Home. The name was appropriate. The mortuary looked like a plantation house. Massive white fluted columns soared two stories or more from the wide porch. The grass out front looked like green carpet had been rolled out. It was beautiful, but out of place. The area around the fancy-looking building had declined to rows of grassless, trash-strewn yards, houses with peeling paint and crumbling steps, boarded up businesses and busted sidewalks. For the first time since she had started walking, Brenda felt anxious. Her pace had slowed considerably, and she was tired. She looked around. *All kinds of people are out walking. I'll be okay.* She wasn't sure if it was the neighborhood or the funeral home that made her nervous. Regardless, Brenda picked up her pace. She began to grow more anxious as the sun got lower in the sky. *It's getting' dark, and I ain't even made it out of Eubanks County. I bet Curtis is wondering where I'm at. I'm gonna have to get me a ride.*

But Brenda was afraid to stick out her thumb. *What if somebody crazy stopped and tried to pick me up? What if one of them big transfer trucks zoomed by and knocked me off my feet?*

The questions mounted, and Brenda began having trouble putting her thoughts together. She needed to concentrate, but the harder she tried, the less successful she was and the more upset she became. She knew what she was doing. She knew where she was going, but her mind was fighting her left and right. She started crying.

A Georgia State Patrolman caught sight of a clearly agitated Brenda. He drove slowly past her in his blue and silver car and watched her in his rear-view mirror. She appeared red faced; she was crying and unsteady on her feet. He pulled over and waited for her to approach.

The officer radioed in. "Dispatch, I've got a white female in apparent distress and possibly under the influence walking on Highway 53, headed toward Hugo. Suspect is approaching on foot."

The patrolman turned on his blue lights.

The lights startled Brenda. She dropped her head and tried to pick up her pace, but she couldn't seem to make her feet do what she wanted them to do. *Walk! Just walk!*

Her mouth felt dry. She hadn't thought to bring water with her. She hadn't packed a snack either. She was thirsty and weak.

Walk, Brenda Lee! Walk! The voice inside her head took on a different sound. It was no longer hers, but Curtis's. *Come on, now. You've got to get to Knoxville tonight. People is waiting on you.*

"Ma'am, do you need help?" the patrolman called out.

"No!" Brenda said abruptly and far too loudly. She had never been stopped by a policeman before. "I'm going to Knoxville."

"Ma'am?"

"I'm going to … to Knoxville, to the World's … Fair," she said. It was getting harder to understand the patrolman and harder for her to put her words together. She didn't recognize what was happening. Her own voice sounded like it was at the other end of a tunnel. Her feet wouldn't cooperate, and she couldn't do anything about it. Her sugar was dropping. The 10-mile walk in the Georgia heat had soaked her pretty blouse with the pink roses, and the polyester pants felt hotter than she ever remembered.

"Ma'am, Knoxville, Tennessee is a good four hours by car. It'll take you a week to get there on foot. Are you sure I can't help you?"

"Curtis Whitfield is…Whoop!" Brenda caught herself. It was the first time in two decades that she had said his name out loud to anyone other than Curtis himself.

"I shouldn't have said that," Brenda said, far too loudly, an erratic giggle escaping her mouth.

"It's okay ma'am. You want to tell me about this Curtis Whitfield? Is he your husband? Are you in trouble?"

Brenda's laugh, fueled by dehydration and low blood sugar, was now more of a cackle. The patrolman made a mental note to be on alert.

"No, he ain't my husband, and no I ain't in trouble!" Brenda said, again too loudly. "I ain't married! I'm just going to see the windmills."

"The windmills ma'am?"

"The Australian windmills."

"Ma'am?"

"At the World's Fair. The windmills at the World's Fair."

"OK ma'am. How 'bout you gettin' in the car with me and let me take you home. It's getting' late."

"No!" Brenda hollered. "I've got to get to Knoxville. Cur- *somebody's* expecting me. Besides, I can't go home. Daddy will be so mad at me, and my brother will too."

"Ma'am, I don't think you're well. Is there somebody else I can call? Can I call this Curtis Whitfield for you?"

Well, yes you can! I've got his number right... Somewhere in the fog of exhaustion and low blood sugar, Brenda suddenly realized that she didn't have a number for Curtis. She had no way of contacting him when she got to Knoxville. *How would he even know I was there?*

A sense of despair, futility and shame washed over her. She couldn't call Curtis. He had always called her. She didn't have an address for him either. They were going to meet at the World's Fair. Brenda was in trouble. She couldn't call Curtis. She was too embarrassed to call Miss Edna or Rogene. She wouldn't call Robert or her daddy. Brenda Lee Branch was all alone, just like the night her mama died.

Salty tears stung eyes already raw from the day's journey. The patrolman opened the door to the back of the patrol car. Brenda collapsed onto the seat, her legs not quite reaching the ground.

"Can you take me home?" she asked.

CHAPTER 14
EUBANKS COUNTY HOSPITAL

The State Patrolman didn't take Brenda home.

He turned off his blue lights and got Brenda settled in the back of his patrol car, then radioed in that he would be transporting Brenda Lee Branch, white female, age 44, to the emergency room at Eubanks County Hospital in Paris.

Brenda was sinking fast. She had sugar tablets in her purse, but she couldn't see it. *"Where's my pocketbook and my suitcase?"* She had lost the ability to communicate, but her brain screamed.

The patrolman glanced back at her, then spoke to her, his eyes searching for Brenda's in the rear-view mirror. She stared blankly ahead.

To help his passenger stay calm, the patrolman turned on the radio to an AM station playing oldies from way back. Connie Francis' pure, mournful voice was just loud enough to drown out the patrol car's motor and just soft enough to be a sad lullaby for Brenda.

Who's sorry now?
Who's sorry now?
Whose heart is achin' for breakin' each vow?
Who's sad and blue, who's cryin' too?
Just like I cried over you.
Right to the end, just like a friend,
I tried to warn you somehow.
You had your way, now you must pay.
I'm glad that you're sorry now.

After the ER staff got her stabilized, Brenda was transferred to the Eubanks County Behavioral Hospital. A full day of rest, nutrition and hydration helped her body to recover, but it took two more days for the fog in her brain to clear. Brenda spent the better part of those three days keeping to herself, watching the other patients and avoiding any mention of Knoxville, the World's Fair or Curtis Whitfield.

I'm not like them. I'm not crazy. My sugar got low, that's all. She kept these thoughts to herself, though she truly didn't understand why she was there. The staff didn't seem to appreciate her perfectly reasonable explanation for being up on Highway 53.

Their probing looks and nods felt a lot like disapproval and not at all understanding.

At night, the patients in the behavioral hospital had rooms to themselves. Though she missed her own bed, the two nights she spent there were at least tolerable. The days were hard, harder than 8 hours at the cotton mill could ever have been. The patients spent the daylight hours in carefully supervised community groups, where they could interact with one another. Part of that time was spent in counseling or group therapy, and that was okay, she reckoned, but the times when nothing was planned, where Brenda and the other patients were together in one big day room, scared her.

Most of the time, she opted to stay close to the wall, her arms folded across her chest. From there, she could see a girl, maybe 18 or 19, who chose to sit in a vinyl-covered chair in the corner with her legs drawn up, her knees touching her chest. She rocked back and forth silently, her arms wrapped around and squeezing her legs. Her hair looked like it hadn't been combed, and her hospital gown was way too big for her. *She looks as lost as a Bessie bug*, Brenda thought. She wondered if that poor girl rocked like that all night.

During group counseling time, an older lady with wild gray hair dominated the conversation. Brenda didn't like her voice, or her words. She talked like she had swallowed sandpaper, and she started or ended every sentence by taking the good Lord's name in vain. No matter what the therapist said to the group, the woman interrupted her with her foul mouth. Her gravelly voice set Brenda's already fragile nerves further on edge. *That woman ain't crazy,* Brenda decided. *She's possessed!*

Two men were also in her group. One of them reminded her of her daddy. He mostly grunted. She didn't know why he was there, but she overheard a nurse say his family never came to see him. That didn't sound good. She steered clear of him.

The other man was *younger and had a bad weight problem*, as she would later describe him. Brenda knew it wasn't polite to stare, but honest to goodness, she had never seen anybody that size in her whole life. It took everything she had in her not to ask him about it. She thought he caught her looking at him more than once. She couldn't help herself. She wondered how he got to the hospital, and she was about to ask a nurse until she remembered how she got there. She didn't want people to know she had come in the back of Georgia State Patrol car. He probably didn't want people to know how he got there either. She'd just have to keep wondering.

The therapy lady kept asking Brenda questions about Curtis and her plans to visit Knoxville. Brenda kept telling her she didn't want to talk about it, and she didn't. *I do not want to talk to a perfect stranger about Curtis Whitfield, and I do not want to talk to you about the World's Fair.*

"I aint' got nothing to say," Brenda told her. "I just need to get home so I can cook supper for daddy and Robert and get back to work." She didn't admit feeling embarrassed and lonely or that the surge of hope she'd begun to feel the previous week had faded to nothing.

Brenda didn't have any answers for the therapist. She had questions of her own.

Was Curtis waiting on her?

Did the girls at the beauty shop know where she was?

What was her daddy and brother gonna say?

Was she in trouble with the law?

What would she tell Miss Edna and Rogene?

The flood of questions exhausted her. She just wanted to sleep in her own bed, sagging mattress and all. If she could just curl up in her bedroom, covered by the threadbare yellow chenille bedspread that had been

her mama's, she'd be okay. But she couldn't do that, not yet.

Leroy Branch didn't go see his daughter while she was in the hospital. Neither did Robert, or Miss Edna or Rogene. Nobody. Brenda couldn't blame them. She didn't know if they even knew where she was. She hadn't told any of them about her plans out of fear they'd try to talk her out of her plan or even stop her from going. If they had found out what had happened, she guessed she probably had hurt their feelings or, worse, disappointed them. Brenda didn't like to disappoint people.

On the day she was discharged, her daddy walked into the office where Brenda waited with a nurse, a counselor and the paperwork lady.

"Did y'all shock her?" Leroy asked. She hated that he acted like she wasn't even in the room, but she'd never tell him that. "We had to do that one time before."

Brenda looked down at the floor.

What did he mean? Shocked, like in the head? Had she had been shocked before? Her daddy must have been confused. She had never been shocked, had she? Wouldn't she remember something like that? *Maybe not. Maybe you don't remember when you've been shocked.* Her mind was racing with questions, but something told her to keep her questions to herself. She just really, really wanted to go home.

The nurse said doctors had not used ECT on Brenda this time.

This time? Brenda said to herself. *What did that mean?*

Brenda had received a sedative, fluids, sugar and insulin, and she had recovered just fine. The nurse told Brenda's daddy that her biggest issue when she came to the hospital was dehydration and that he needed to make sure she was drinking plenty of water.

She listened as the counselor talked to her daddy like she was some kid who couldn't think for herself. *I am not a kid.* The counselor told him Brenda was in a fragile state, that she needed rest and that she needed to take her medicine. She repeated these same things to Brenda, like she hadn't heard them the first time, and asked her to confirm that she understood. Brenda lowered her head, looked at the floor and nodded.

I understand. I understand that I am a 44-year-old woman who can answer my own questions and make my own decisions. I understand that I make my own money. Her thoughts made her angry, but the anger was quickly followed by resignation. *I understand that I can't even make it out of Eubanks County on my own. I understand that daddy and Robert expect me to cook their meals and have it on the table, clean their house and wash their clothes. I let them down. I let mama down.*

If people could shrink, Brenda was positive that she had. She felt small, like a mouse trapped in a corner.

"I just want to go home," Brenda told them.

With the paperwork signed, her belongings returned, and instructions received, the only thing between Brenda and the bed she longed for was the 20-minute drive home with her daddy. Neither of them said a word. It would have been nice to have something playing on the radio, even Paul Harvey, but her daddy had the radio turned off.

It was the longest ride of her life.

CHAPTER 15
HOME WHERE I BELONG

Brenda was so tired from her long walk to Paris and her short stay in the hospital that she was having trouble concentrating. Her brain silently spit out one-word ideas as her daddy drove toward Sumner.

Work.

Supper.

Robert.

Curtis.

Fist fight.

World's Fair.

State Patrolman.

Blue lights.

Beauty shop.

Miss Edna.

Church.

Mama.

Daddy.

Embarrassed.

Leroy pulled onto the packed gravel driveway beside the house and stopped. Brenda didn't move. This had been the only place she had ever lived that she could remember. She should have felt comforted, welcomed or appreciative, but she didn't. She just felt…empty.

Leroy got out of the car and went straight to the house. He paused at the front door and looked back at Brenda, still sitting in the car. He shrugged and went inside. Leroy was not equipped to deal with female trouble, crazy-headed ideas or wild hairs. A long time ago he would have prayed about it, but he hadn't prayed since Viola died a lifetime ago.

CHAPTER 16
LEROY AND VIOLA

Leroy Branch had met Viola Godfrey in 1933. Viola – everybody who knew her pronounced it VY-ola, had just started working at the cotton mill in Sumner, and Leroy, who was four years older, got assigned to train her. At 16, Viola was the tiniest little thing Leroy had ever seen. At 5-foot, 2-inches tall, every feature was petite. He didn't think she'd last a day in the mill, but she did. In fact, she worked circles around most of the men.

It didn't take long before Leroy started calling on Viola at her mama's house, and after about a year of courting, he asked her to marry him. Viola accepted his proposal, and with the approval of her daddy, the pair got married before a Justice of the Peace in Paris. They didn't go on a fancy honeymoon or even stay in a motel in Paris. After the wedding they promptly drove back to Sumner in time for their shifts at the mill.

Robert came along a couple of years later, and Brenda arrived next, right at two years later. Ed Earl was the last Branch child, for which Viola felt grateful. Ed Earl had been a difficult pregnancy, and his breach position made his delivery far harder than Robert and Brenda had been combined. The youngest Branch came out of the womb with a loud, demanding cry, a foreshadow of his ability to command attention from the pulpits he filled.

Leroy had not been a church-going man when he met Viola, but her daddy insisted that he attend church if he wanted to court his daughter. Leroy started going to services, and one Sunday, felt the pull of the Holy Ghost on his heart. Leroy went to the altar in a heap of tears, surrounded by Viola's daddy and a mountain of deacons. But he didn't fully meet the qualification of marrying Alton Godfrey's baby girl. Her daddy insisted that Leroy be baptized, full immersion, all-the-way under, every-hair-on-his-head wet as a public acknowledgement that he was "buried with Jesus in baptism and raised to walk in the newness of life," as the preacher explained it. Leroy came out of the water fully wet, fully changed and fully ready to start a new life with the girl who had stolen his heart.

After the wedding, Leroy and Viola continued to show up at church every Wednesday night and twice on Sunday. And when Robert, Brenda and Ed Earl came along, they took the kids with them. Church was as central to their lives as the mill was until 1965, the year Viola died. Leroy dutifully braved the church doors for Viola's funeral, but he never set foot in a church again.

When their boy, Ed Earl, felt the call to preach, you'd have thought Leroy would have gone to hear him, but he didn't. Brenda went, of course, she never stopped going to church. The Good Book talks about a childlike faith, and Leroy reckoned Brenda had it. It seemed right to her to go and listen to Ed Earl at the little churches where he preached, but Leroy didn't think it seemed right at all. Nothing had seemed right since his wife had died. He didn't reckon going and listening to Ed Earl scream and holler would help.

He might not have prayed, but Leroy had kept one small connection to his faith. He required that the radio in the kitchen stay tuned to Viola's favorite gospel music station, although he would be the first to tell you that this wasn't him holding on to Jesus. This was Leroy trying to hold on to Viola. He might turn the volume down when there was a Braves game or a radio preacher on, but he didn't mind the singing. The old hymns and Southern Gospel quartets reminded him of the life he had built with Miss Viola Godfrey.

Though Viola had been gone a long time, most days it seemed like it was just yesterday that she cooked for her family, sang in the church choir or served with her Eastern Star sisters. Now it was just him, Brenda and Robert living in the same mill house Viola had kept, and things seemed to be falling apart.

Leroy hadn't cried since Viola had gone to meet her Maker, but the events of the past few days were getting to him. If Viola had been here, she'd have known what to do, what to say. She'd have noticed Brenda acting up. If there was ever a time when he needed Viola by his side, it was now.

Now, with Brenda home from the hospital and Robert sullen and distant, he went to the only place he knew to go. Leroy walked into the kitchen and turned up the volume on Viola's old radio.

"Rock of Ages, cleft for me,
Let me hide myself in Thee;
Let the water and the blood,
From Thy riven side which flowed,

Be of sin the double cure,
Save me from its guilt and power.

"Not the labor of my hands
Can fulfill They law's demands;
Could my zeal no respite know,
Could my tears forever flow,
All could never sin erase,
Thou must save and save by grace.

"Nothing in my hands I bring,
Simply to Thy cross I cling;
Naked, come to Thee for dress,
Helpless, look to Thee for grace:
Foul, I to the fountain fly,
Wash me, Savior, or I die."

Brenda sat in the car a long time, still trying to get her thoughts together. *What day is it? Monday? Tuesday?* She didn't know. How many days' work had she missed? *Oh Lord, do I still have a job?* She wasn't one to miss work, but you never could tell about a job. She figured not too many people were clamoring for mill work these days, still, the thought gave her something else to worry about. She would have entertained that worry, but her stomach growled. It was getting close to supper time, and supper wasn't going to cook itself.

Brenda sighed, opened the car door and stood. She felt about as wobbly as a congealed salad at a church homecoming. Brenda steadied herself, retrieved her purse and suitcase from the back seat, then walked in the house and straight to her bedroom. She put her suitcase and pocketbook on her bed and then proceeded to the kitchen. Leroy knew he probably needed to say something, but he didn't know what to say.

"I wondered if we's gonna have anything t' eat tonight," he said from the living room, where he had settled into an old recliner. At least that was something.

"It's OK, daddy. I'm about to start frying some chicken livers," Brenda said softly, tying her mama's yellow apron around her waist.

"Chicken livers! Today ain't Monday. What's got into you girl?" Leroy was lost. Rather than risk Brenda crying on him, or her starting a conversation about missing her mama, he decided to keep the conversation as safe as possible.

Her daddy's questions settled one of Brenda's own. It wasn't Monday. It must be Tuesday. She had forgotten to count the night she spent in the emergency room.

"Did I say chicken livers? I meant salmon patties. I'll get to work on the salmon right now."

Leroy nodded and settled into his well-worn brown Naugahyde recliner in the living room. Over the years, Leroy's body had shaped the chair until it precisely fit on him, although nothing looked very precise about it anymore. The Branches bought the chair new in 1961, and no one had ever sat in it since the day Leroy and Robert lifted it off the truck bed. The padded arms had faded and cracked indentions opened where he rested his elbows. There was a similar spot right where Leroy reclined his head. Two faded and cracked ovals on the footrest supported his sock-covered heels. The Braves were playing on TV—Ted Turner's Channel 17 Superstation from Atlanta. Brenda knew her daddy never liked to talk when the Braves were on, and that was fine with both of them. Hopefully, the game would let him off the hook for talking to her and shield Brenda from the questions she didn't want to answer.

Brenda turned the volume down on Viola's radio and started preparing the vegetables. After peeling and slicing the carrots, she put them in a boiler with some sugar and water. She didn't measure the sugar. She got a dinner spoon–Brenda called it a tablespoon–and stuck it deep into the sugar jar. She pulled out a heaping mound of white crystals and stirred it into the now-steaming water.

She got out her mama's old iron skillet and set it on the stove with a pour of Mazola in it. Her mama had never used cooking oil. She would have used lard, but one day at the Piggly Wiggly, Brenda had bought a bottle of Mazola oil on a whim, and she liked it. Neither Leroy nor Robert, who had come in after she had started fixin' supper, seemed to notice or care. From that point on, she had used Mazola. It was a little victory from 10 years ago, but sometimes it seemed like little victories were about all she had.

The only sounds in the house were sizzling salmon patties and the Braves' play-by-play. This left Brenda alone with her thoughts at a time she didn't want to be. Brenda thought about turning the radio volume back up, but she knew Leroy didn't like the sound to interfere with his baseball games. Besides, she wasn't in the mood to hear *Rise Again* for the umpteenth time. The Christian deejays had been playing Dallas Holm nonstop. *I can't take it no more if*

I hear that man sing about driving nails in Jesus' hands one more time.

Instead, she focused on the Braves, who were doing pretty good that spring. They were playing the Dodgers. Ken Dayley was pitching. Leroy liked Dayley OK, but he'd never match Phil Niekro. Niekro had pitched the Braves to victory the night before. Brenda didn't know who either of them was, but if her daddy liked Niekro, she reckoned she did too.

When the hushpuppies were done, Brenda called her daddy and Robert into the kitchen, with an exhausted, "Supper's ready."

The men sat down at the chrome dinette table and waited for Brenda to hand them their plates. She spooned carrots onto the avocado-colored melamine plates, added a stack of salmon patties and three hushpuppies.

After fixing her own plate, she sat the ketchup bottle down in the middle of the table, and the three of them ate in silence. The only sound was the rattle of stainless forks and spoons clattering on plastic. There was plenty to talk about, but nobody knew what to say, and each was thankful that no one tried to start a conversation.

After supper, Brenda started soaking the pinto beans for Wednesday's supper. She finished cleaning up the kitchen while Gene Garber finished pitching the top of the 9th for the Braves who beat the Dodgers 4-3. Another victory for the day.

Brenda headed to the bathroom to prepare for bed, and for the first time since she had put on her pink rose blouse, she saw herself in the mirror. Her eyes appeared weak and vacant. The unfamiliar t-shirt she wore didn't belong to her, and she had no idea where it had come from. Her hair looked a mess—with five more days before her regular appointment at the beauty shop, and she looked like she'd stood all night in a rainstorm.

She tried to plump her hair back into some semblance of a style and stopped, realizing that, for the first time in 26 years, there was not a single trace of blue lint in her hair on a weeknight.

Brenda cried herself to sleep.

CHAPTER 17
HENRY

Brenda slept hard that night but woke up still tired. Not that it mattered. Just as sure as Tuesday was salmon night, Wednesday was another workday. She could have used another day to rest, but she figured that wasn't an option. *You can't take a good job for granted.* She could hear her mama's voice saying those very words to her. *I know, Mama. I know.*

She and Robert rode together to the mill. Neither spoke. If her brother had something to say about her failed attempt to reach Knoxville, she hoped he'd keep it to himself. She hoped he wouldn't ask questions either. He didn't. Never married and seldom kissed, Robert didn't want to talk to his sister about anything related to romance. Like his daddy, he had no idea what to say. In public, Robert was alternately dismissive and fiercely protective of his sister. In private, they seldom talked at all, even across the supper table. If anyone ever attempted to get the two oldest Branch children to talk, Robert would grow sullen, drop his chin and mutter, "She's crazy."

At the mill, Brenda clocked in and walked straight into the constant noise of the spooling room. She knew people were looking at her, but most of the folks who worked there seldom talked to her. Brenda didn't take it personally, at least not usually. It's loud in the mill and hard to carry on any kind of decent conversation. People kept to themselves because of the noise, she figured. So, she doubted they'd say anything to her now.

When she first went to work at the mill, she wasn't sure she'd make it there. The rhythmic, deafening sound of the machinery quickly wore on her nerves, and there was no escaping it.

"You'll get used to it," her trainer had told her when she'd started. "Before long, it'll just fade into the background. It'll be so quiet when you get home, you won't hardly be able to stand it."

Brenda couldn't imagine missing the constant ear assault.

Her trainer advised her to ignore the drone, but she couldn't. On that first day 26 years ago, she'd felt every vibration from the top of her head to the bottom of her feet. It was more than sound, it was bone-rattling, chest-tightening and relentless. Brenda couldn't concentrate. She couldn't make her hands do what they were supposed to do. They were trembling. Her whole body was shaking. Overwhelmed, tears spilled from her eyes. The walls were closing in. She was lost, alone, useless.

Her trainer noticed and took her to the break room.

"Do you trust me?" he asked.

Brenda didn't think she had a choice. She nodded.

He went to his lunch box and pulled out a small brown bottle of spirit of ammonia. He took the top off his Thermos and filled it with water at a water fountain, then poured about a teaspoon of the clear liquid from the bottle into the water.

"This is gonna smell bad and taste worse, but I promise you, it'll help," he said. "It's a family recipe."

Brenda didn't care how it tasted or how it smelled, she needed help. She couldn't keep going like this.

She could smell the ammonia. She took a sip, expecting it to burn like alcohol, like the homemade cough medicine her mama had given her growing up.

Instead, it was bitter and dry. The smell took her breath.

She hesitated.

"It's best to drink it as fast as you can," her trainer told her.

Brenda gulped the rest of the liquid and chased it with another Thermos lid of water. Within 20 minutes she was as calm as a pond on a still day. Her nerves settled, she went back into the mill. The sounds of the looms grew fainter. She could work. Brenda never really noticed the mill sounds much after that, but she was always careful to keep a little ammonia with her just in case her nerves got a hold of her again, and they sometimes did.

Coming back to work felt an awful lot like that first day, and Brenda was genuinely surprised she didn't notice the noisy machinery. If anything, she found sanctuary in the familiarity. At lunch, Brenda sat down at the table she and Miss Edna usually shared. Miss Edna joined her, pulling out a Tupperware container of leftover roast beef, carrots and potatoes. Brenda had made herself a baloney sandwich and filled a plastic baggie with her favorite Ruffles potato chips.

Their 30-minute lunch break was nearly over before Brenda said anything.

"I love him," Brenda said to her friend, before quickly taking a bite of her sandwich.

"Oh, Hon." Miss Edna wasn't one for showing much sympathy, but this was just plain sad. "You remember what that woman on Paul Harvey said? You don't need an ol' man."

"No, I guess I don't," Brenda said, "but it might be nice to have one."

The buzzer sounded. It was time to go back to the spools, where Brenda would be alone with that thought for the next four hours. There was no time to talk about Curtis, the World's Fair, her hospital stay or love. Maybe it was for the best.

Not long after she had gotten home, Brenda heard a quick set of rapid knocks at the door, rattling the screen door that kept the bugs out but allowed the breeze in.

"Hey Miss Brenda? You home? Mama said fer me to come and bring you these cookies."

Brenda quick-stepped to the front door where 8-year-old Henry Williams stood, holding an orange plastic container covered by a yellow sunburst lid.

Brenda smiled and opened the door for Henry to come in.

"Why don't you come in here to the kitchen with me and help me eat one of these cookies?" Brenda asked. She liked for her young neighbors to visit. It brightened her days, and she didn't know why, but she seemed to understand kids better than she did their parents.

"Mama said for me not to do that," Henry said. "She said you might not be feeling good."

"I feel alright, Hon. I'm just a little tired from working all day, but that's nothing that a bite of one of your mama's cookies won't fix."

Brenda poured them both a glass of sweet milk, removed the lid of the bowl and told Henry to take the first pick.

Henry chose the biggest one and took a bite, and, with his mouth still full, said "Mama said you was in the hospital."

"I was, baby," Brenda said, "but I'm okay now."

"She said you was in the crazy hospital."

Brenda bit her bottom lip. Henry didn't know that he shouldn't say things like that, but his mama did. *She ought to know better than to talk about such things in front of a kid. If you ever want to know what people are really saying about you, ask a kid. They know plenty, they hear plenty, and they don't know what not to tell you. Maybe that's why I like kids better. They're honest, and you don't have to worry about them stabbing you in the back.*

"Well, baby, that ain't exactly true, but it ain't a lie neither. What matters is that I feel a whole lot better now that you brought me these cookies. Did you help your mama make 'em?

"I got the sugar out for my mama to use," Henry told her, crumbs falling.

"Well, that's why these taste so good," enjoying the cookie as much as the boy.

Henry grinned a broad grin. He had been Brenda's next-door neighbor for about two years. His mama, Laney, worked third shift at the mill. That meant she could get home just in time to see Henry and his baby sister off to school, sleep while they were at school and work while they were sleeping. Henry's daddy, Jeff, was in the service, stationed in Germany. Laney had moved her family to Sumner to be close to her husband's mama and daddy. She needed them to help her and her kids while her husband was serving his country overseas.

Sometimes, Henry would bring his little sister, Shelby, with him. They usually didn't come when Leroy or Robert was at home. She figured her daddy and brother scared them. Sometimes Henry would bring a ball or a toy car to play with. Brenda would have him sit in the floor with his legs spread wide. Brenda would sit across the room in the same position, and they'd roll the ball or the car back and forth to each other. Shelby sometimes brought her baby doll or her Barbie doll over. Brenda liked it when she did. She and Shelby would bathe and dress the baby doll, getting it ready for night-night. Or they would fix Barbie's hair for her date that night with Ken. Every once in a while, Henry would ask Brenda to help him with his homework. Brenda was good reader and a pretty good mathematician. She liked helping him, and she was excited about this next school year. Henry would be learning his times tables. Brenda could still remember the orange and white multiplication tables she got when she was in third grade. She had memorized them all the way and could still recite them through the 11s without missing a beat. She used to could do the 12s, but they had gotten harder to recall in recent years.

Henry finished his cookie and told Brenda he had to get back home.

"Did you save out a cookie for Shelby, Hon?" she asked.

Henry nodded.

"Okay, but if that cookie gets gone, you tell Shelby to come on over here and eat one with Miss Brenda, alright?"

Henry smiled.

"Okay!" Henry was out the door and running across the yard, cookie in hand.

Brenda took two of the cookies and put them in sandwich bag for work tomorrow. She'd share one with Miss Edna. She'd like that. She left the rest on the counter. They wouldn't be there tomorrow once her daddy and Robert saw them, but that was OK. *Maybe leaving them a little something sweet will start to pay them back for the trouble I caused.*

CHAPTER 18
MEET ROBERT BRANCH

Robert Branch was not a bad man, but he was not a good man either. He lived with his daddy and helped with his sister, not because he had compassion, but out of duty. Besides, he had no other options. As soon as he and Brenda cashed their checks each week, he put $25 in a plain envelope, gave Leroy money for groceries and utilities and quickly gambled the rest away in late night poker games at the back of Stanley's shop, where he rarely walked away a winner. He saw his life and the Sumner mill house he shared with Leroy and Brenda as a prison of his own making, and he had been bitter about it just about every day of his adult life.

It hadn't always been this way for Robert. Back in the 50s, he had been a decent baseball player, and he had hoped his skill would take him to the big leagues. But a pregnant girl and his habit of gambling had cost Robert all his options. So, like his daddy and granddaddy before him, Robert worked at the mill and lived what was, in his own estimation, a miserable existence.

He had not loved the girl he got pregnant. The baby was conceived in a night of passion during a football game. It was October, and Robert had brought a blanket into the stands, hoping a shivering co-ed would snuggle up next to him. His plan worked. Robert wasn't bad lookin,' and the two left their seats to make out underneath the stands. The couple got carried away, and there, beneath the feet of Sumner, Robert sealed his fate.

Robert and the girl didn't see each other again, not until her daddy caught up with him one April night at Stanley's.

"Is Robert Branch in there?" the girl's daddy hollered out.

"Who's asking?" Robert hollered back.

"Jim Acres," the voice hollered back.

"I don't know no Jim Acres," Robert replied, "and you gonna have to wait. I'm 'bout to win this hand."

"You're about to lose your life," Jim Acres replied. "You best get out here NOW!"

Robert laid his cards down and slid his seat back. He and the rest of the boys walked outside where Jim Acres waited with his two oldest boys, Junior and Tad. The three of them were carrying baseball bats.

"Whoa now," Robert said. "What's this all about?"

Robert might have been a gambler, but he wasn't no troublemaker.

"You got my baby girl pregnant, and you're gonna pay, boy" Jim Acres said.

"Mister, I don't know what you're talking about. I ain't been messin' around with no gal."

"Carol Lynn! Come here!"

A young girl with a round belly slipped out of a pickup truck and into the dim pool of light cast by the single bulb above Stanley's door.

"Yes sir?"

Robert's face went white. He couldn't keep himself from staring at the girl's growing stomach.

"Is this the boy that…had his way with you?"

"Yes sir."

"Look here now," Robert said, "how I'm supposed to know I'm the only man your girl's been with."

"You sayin' my girl sleeps around like a two-bit Jezebel?" Jim Acres pulled the baseball bat in his hands back behind his right shoulder.

"No sir, I'm not. I'm just wondering what kind of proof you have that I'm the cause of, of THAT." Robert pointed to Carol Lynn's belly.

"Robert," Carol Lynn said, looking down at her slowly disappearing feet. "I ain't been with nobody else. The baby is yours."

Robert sighed. He knew he was the father, and he knew that his life would never be the same.

At 19-years-old, Robert was a man. He would handle this.

He and Jim agreed to meet in Paris. There was no need for Sumner's prying eyes and ears to get wind of this. They met at a café on the north end of town and sat in a booth in the back corner.

Carol Lynn had withdrawn from high school. She was going to a home for pregnant girls in South Carolina. She'd finish her studies there, have the baby and leave it in Spartanburg with Jim's youngest sister. Then, Carol Lynn would go off to college or secretarial school. By the time she came back to Sumner, she'd be ready for a job, and people wouldn't have a second thought about it.

Jim told Robert what he would do.

He would give up his baseball dream and quit gambling. He would quit hanging out at Stanley's. He would work hard at his job. He would send $25 a week to Jim Acres, who would deposit the money into an account for the grandbaby he would never acknowledge.

Robert agreed to Jim's requirements. What choice did he have? He told no one about Jim, Carol Lynn or the baby—not his mama, not his daddy, nobody. He went to the mill the next day and got a job, the job he would keep until he retired.

Robert hated the mill. He hated the rhythmic drone of the machines. He hated the blue lint in his hair. Robert Branch's boyhood sin had chained him down. He'd never be able to run the bases tethered to a baby he'd never meet and a machine he despised. He was serving a life sentence in the West Oaks cotton mill, with no hope of pardon for his tortured soul, no matter what the preacher said.

To cover his need to get money to Jim Acres, Robert told his daddy he wanted to set up a bank account in Paris to put a little money back for the future. Leroy, proud of his son's mature decision, never questioned him. Of course, Robert didn't have a bank account. Jim Acres did. And the money wasn't for his future, it was for Carol Lynn's baby. Even now, every Friday, Robert goes to Paris to cash his check and send $25 to a kid he'd never meet.

Robert didn't gamble, at least not for a year or so, but he eventually landed back at Stanley's. Old habits die hard, they say. Luckily, he still lived at home. When he paid his rightful share, he, his daddy and Brenda made enough to keep the house running. The rest he could do with as he liked.

It didn't occur to Robert that he could leave. He could've gotten a place in Paris or quit the mill and moved to Atlanta. Ed Earl could've helped take care of Brenda and their daddy, but blinded by a remorse that had quickly turned to resentment, Robert didn't see those options. When Carol Lynn's daddy laid down the law that night at Stanley's, Robert had accepted the shackles around his ankles and assumed Jim Acres had thrown away the key.

CHAPTER 19
MEET ED EARL BRANCH

From the day he was born Ed Earl Branch was a screamer. As a baby, he would take a big gasp of air and let out a blood-curdling scream. You could hear Ed Earl's cry all the way to the railroad tracks. As a preacher, he did the same.

His Sunday morning sermons at Mt. Carmel Primitive Baptist Church usually began with Ed Earl crying. He couldn't help it. He loved singing out of the red back *Church Hymns* book that populated the backs of every pew, and once the song leader started, Ed Earl was done for. Whether it was *Victory in Jesus* or *I Surrender All,* Ed Earl would be sniffing back tears, and Lord forbid that the song leader pulled out *Just As I Am* or *Amazing Grace.* There was no coming back from that, Ed Earl would be a sobbing mess, voice cracking, nose running and tears flowing.

Ed Earl stood behind the oak pulpit and pulled out his wadded-up white handkerchief.

"You know the Lord is good."

"Amen!"

"He saved me when I was just a boy no bigger than this young man." Ed Earl pointed to a 10-year-old fidgeting on the second pew. "I knew I was a dirty sinner, Brother David. I knew it."

"AMEN brother!"

The tears resumed, and Ed Earl's voice wavered.

"I was dirty sinner, and Jesus said He'd take me just as I am. Just as I am, Brother!"

"Just as you are!"

The tears were now pouring, and Ed Earl was beside himself.

"There I was, without one plea, Sister Ellen! But you know what?"

His voice trailed off, and the congregation grew quiet.

"Jesus' blood was shed for me," Ed Earl whispered.

"AMEN!"

"Preach it!"

"Tell 'em brother!"

With the prompting of the congregation, all 30 or so of them, Ed Earl took a deep breath, and the preaching commenced.

"And I, hah, tell you, hah! Jesus, hah, is The Way, hah, The Truth, hah, and The Life, hah! No man, hah, cometh to The Father, hah, but by Him, hah!

"You can try the beer joints, hah, but that ain't the way, hah! You can try women, hah, but that ain't the way! You, hah, can try, hah, buying a fancy car, hah, but that ain't the way, hah!

Ed Earl took a big breath of air and exclaimed, "I'm a-tellin' you, Brother David, JESUS IS THE WAY!"

"HALLELUJAH!"

"PRAISE THE LORD!"

"THANK YOU, JESUS!"

"AMEN!"

It was Wednesday night, and Ed Earl could feel the move of the Holy Ghost. Maybe his heart was a little more tender than other nights. His sister, his poor sister, was in the congregation. She looked lost.

He prayed that she had not strayed from the Lord when she went chasing after a sorry man to a godforsaken place like the World's Fair. Who knew what kind of heathens were selling their idols there?

Brenda Lee knew better. Their mama had raised them better than that. But that's how the ol' devil works. He takes something ugly and makes it look pretty. He turns your head with carnal thoughts, and before you know it, you're walking to Knoxville, chasing a man.

"Jesus is the way, you know," Ed Earl said. He was staring straight at his sister. "And He's right here. He's not in some grand hotel or in a big shiny ball bigger than the sun. No, He's right here." Ed Earl tapped his chest with his right index finger.

Brenda looked down at her own chest. She knew the Good Lord was supposed to be in there, but right now she didn't feel much of anything.

The song leader had come back to the front, and sweet little Sandy Smith, who had learned her octaves and chords from her own mama when she couldn't even reach the pedals, had sat down at the piano. It was time for the altar call.

"What can wash away our sins?
Nothing but the blood of Jesus.
What can make us whole again?
Nothing but the blood of Jesus.
Oh, precious is the flow;
That makes us white as snow.

> *Oh, no other fount I know,*
> *Nothing but the blood of Jesus."*

The invitations at the Mt. Carmel Primitive Baptist Church, they called them altar calls, were unpredictable. They always followed the preaching, and there was always a song about sin, surrender or Jesus's blood, but that's where the similarities ended. Sometimes the song leader would only get through one verse and one chorus before the service ended, but if Ed Earl thought somebody needed to come down to the front to pray, he'd keep the song going until the right sinner stood up and met Jesus.

He hoped Brenda would respond to the invitation, but she didn't budge.

"Sing that last verse again, Brother Alan!"

> *"This is all my hope and peace.*
> *Nothing but the blood of Jesus.*
> *This is all my righteousness..."*

"Won't you come?" Ed Earl pleaded. "Won't you come let Jesus wash away your sins?"

> *"Oh, precious is the flow,*
> *that makes me white as snow – oh."*

"Jesus loves you, sister." Ed Earl said. "He can make a black heart whiter than a January snow."

Brenda wasn't singing anymore. She knew what the Bible said about sinning against God, but she wasn't sure whether trying to see Curtis was a sin or just bad planning. *Is it wrong to love?* She knew her heart felt stony and maybe even black. She knew she needed Jesus, but right now, she just felt tired.

After church, Brenda stayed in her pew, waiting for Ed Earl to finish talking to the brothers and sisters in the congregation.

With the last light was out and the double doors locked behind them, Brenda and Ed Earl made their way to the car. Brenda sat in the back seat on the passenger side. Ed Earl's wife, Mary Jo, took the front seat beside her husband, who was driving.

"Good service tonight, Ed Earl," Mary Jo said.

"Thank you, Honey. The Lord was there, wouldn't you say so, Brenda?"

"I reckon he was there," Brenda responded, her voice barely audible. She knew Ed Earl would press in. He wasn't one to leave questions unasked.

"Brenda, you feelin' OK?"

"I reckon."

"I thought you might come up to the altar."

"No. I guess I just didn't know what to pray about."

"The Good Book says that when we don't know what to pray for, the Holy Ghost knows what to pray for us."

"Well, I reckon the Holy Ghost don't need me on my knees to pray for me."

"No, he don't, but the Lord loves a humble heart."

That right there was the problem, Brenda thought. She didn't know if it was possible for her heart to get any lower.

CHAPTER 20
BRENDA LEE BRANCH

Brenda had always needed extra attention. The second child and only daughter of Leroy and Viola Branch was premature and weighed just four pounds when she was born. When baby girl came home from the hospital, Viola had to keep her against her chest or else Brenda would quit breathing. Feeding was another issue entirely. Brenda wasn't strong enough, nor her belly big enough, to take in more than an hour's worth of milk at a time. That meant Viola had to grab catnaps in a rocking chair while holding Brenda gently against her bosom. In between, Viola juggled taking care of Robert, who wasn't yet 3, keeping meals on the table and making passes at dusting, sweeping and mopping. She was exhausted.

Leroy didn't believe in kids sharing a bedroom with their parents, but Viola insisted when Brenda came along. Brenda had been so frail, and Viola had lost so much sleep, that once Brenda was able to sleep by herself, she was not about to let her out of her sight.

Viola fashioned a makeshift bassinet from the bottom drawer of a chest in their bedroom. She emptied the drawer and layered it in quilts and blankets. Every night, Brenda slept in the drawer right at her mama's side, and each day, Viola would slide the drawer back into place to keep things tidy.

Brenda started catching up physically when she was about two years old, but those early years had created a dependency on her mama that would last a lifetime. As she grew, it became apparent that Brenda was, well, *different*. Viola had heard that word whispered about her daughter, but she was always careful to protect her from the stares and muttered comments. Her mama would say she was smart as a whip, whatever that meant. Smart or not, Brenda lived in a sheltered and naïve world that left her both highly emotional and eternally optimistic. It was an odd combination to be sure.

As a toddler, if there was an argument between her brothers, Brenda cried, as bothered by the tension as she was the noise. Later, if the neighbors got into an argument, Brenda worried. When she found a baby bird that fell from its nest, Brenda was positive it would live, grow and become her pet. And when her dog was hit by a car, she had been confident he would heal. Both the bird and the dog died, but Leroy, Viola, Robert and even little Ed Earl conspired to keep that truth from her.

"Robert! You need to come out here," an 8-year-old Ed Earl hollered from outside the window of the bedroom they shared.

Robert, five years older, didn't want to play with his baby brother. "Call Brenda Lee," he said. "She'll play with you."

"Shhhhhh! I need YOU!" Ed Earl said, glancing to the left and right. "Right now!"

Sensing the urgency in his little brother's voice, Robert made his way slowly to Ed Earl, who was squatted down next to the house. He looked troubled.

"What is it?" Robert asked.

Ed Earl raised his head to look at his brother, then slowly held out his hands, which were cupped together. In them was a lifeless wren.

"Put that thing down!" Robert said.

Ed Earl clinched his teeth and whispered angrily.

"This is Brenda Lee's bird, Robert. It died."

"Stay right there." Robert ran and got a shovel, checking the door and the yard to make sure Brenda was nowhere in sight. "Let's take him down the road a piece."

Robert dug a small hole, and the brothers buried the bird.

"You can't say nothin' to Brenda Lee about this," Robert told his brother.

"She loved that little bird," Ed Earl said.

"I know, and that's why we can't tell her," Robert said. "You know Brenda. She can't handle bad news like that."

Ed Earl nodded. He understood.

"I won't say nothin'," he said.

At supper that night, Robert waited for the right moment to launch a story.

"Brenda Lee, you know that ol' bird you was nursing?" Ed Earl looked at his brother, unsure of what the plan was.

"You mean Sally!" Brenda said with a broad smile.

"Well, I reckon she got herself a boyfriend," Robert said. "I saw her fly off today with another bird.

Ed Earl smiled. "It's true Brenda Lee. She looked so happy. I bet they's gonna make a nest together somewhere."

Robert nodded toward his brother. Brenda drank in their words.

"I'm gonna miss her," Brenda said. "But ain't it sweet that she found a boy bird?"

That was Brenda Lee. Naïve. Tenderhearted. Trusting. Believing the best.

That naivety and trust carried over into all facets of Brenda's small world. The Branches were poor, but Brenda never knew it. During lean times, when food was scarce in the cupboard, Brenda learned at her mama's side to make the most of what she had. Viola would cook up a mess of beans, collards and cornbread, giving thanks to the Lord the whole time for such goodness on the table.

"This is soul food, Brenda," Viola would say. "It's good for the soul, and it's good for the heart." Brenda didn't know they were eating pintos because they were poor. She thought her mama was looking out for her family's soul.

When Christmas or her birthday rolled around, Brenda never doubted that she'd get exactly what she had asked for. Mindful of her special nature, Viola and

Leroy seemed always to make sure she received the gift she expected. If not, they were ready with an explanation.

Brenda wasn't greedy. She wouldn't dream of asking for something at the expense of someone else. So, when her mama had explained that Santa had to help a whole lot of children across the world and that she had to limit her list, Brenda didn't mind at all. It just helped her to prioritize. If she didn't get what she had asked for, Brenda's family made sure to keep her from doubting the magic of Christmas.

The hoped-for gift in 1946 was a baby doll whose eyes closed when she was put to bed, but when Brenda checked under the tree that year, there was no doll.

"Hon, I know you wanted that baby doll," Viola said, "but when Santa came in here and told me they was only one left, I knew we couldn't ask him to leave it for you. He told us about a little girl up in Paris whose only doll had been burned in a bad fire. That little girl wanted a baby doll just like the one you wanted, so I told Santa to give it to her. I hope that's OK."

Brenda Lee believed every word of her mama's story.

"Oh mama! I'm so glad you told him that! That little girl needed her way more than I did." Brenda smiled throughout Christmas Day imagining her mama talking to Santa Claus in front of their Christmas tree and thinking about how happy that little girl must be, and she never once mourned her loss.

"Do you think we could go to Paris so maybe I could see how happy that baby doll made that little girl? Maybe we could bring her some of my clothes!"

Viola told her daughter that Santa didn't give her names and addresses, but she knew he'd be mighty proud of such selfless thinking.

Some might say that kind of thinking is a curse, but Brenda's mama saw it as a blessing. When she did begin to notice the heartless ugliness of others, the years of her family's protection had resulted in an innocent optimism that shielded Brenda from name-calling gossips or mean-spirited hoodlums. When people called her or her brothers lint-heads, she quickly turned the hurt into thankfulness that her mama and daddy had jobs. When kids shunned her in the schoolyard, Brenda would volunteer to clean the blackboard or she would pull out a book to read, figuring their game already had enough players.

That same attitude and blind faith carried Brenda all the way into high school. So, when Curtis Whitfield started smiling and winking right at her, Brenda didn't see his rough edges. All she saw was good.

CHAPTER 21
COOKING AND CONJURING

Brenda's first memory of her mama's yellow apron was at Thanksgiving. It was 1943. She would've been five years old, she reckoned.

"Brenda, come in here to the kitchen," Viola called to her daughter. "Tomorrow's Thanksgiving, and I want you to help me make the dinner."

Brenda walked across the worn linoleum floor to her mama, who was standing in front of the white porcelain sink. She was peeling potatoes. Viola pulled a chair from the kitchen table over to the sink, the back against the cabinet.

"Climb up here, little miss. We're gonna make mashed potatoes."

Brenda dutifully climbed up beside her mama. Viola was wearing a yellow apron with pink flowers sprinkled over it. Standing in front of the window, her mama and the apron seemed to glow like angels must—at least that's the way Brenda remembers it now.

"First, we've got to get you an apron! We don't want to mess up our clothes."

Viola opened a drawer and pulled out a neatly folded blue polka dot apron. She tied the strings behind Brenda's neck, then pulled the waist strings to Brenda's waist, allowing the apron to fall against her legs. The apron wrapped completely around Brenda, so her mama tied the strings in front.

"There you go! Now, can you finish washing these potatoes and scrub all the dirt off of them for your mama?"

Brenda nodded vigorously. She watched Viola wash a brown russet, then took a potato for herself and copied her mother's every move until every potato was thoroughly cleaned.

"Next we have to peel them," Viola told her. "Mama's gonna do that part, but I want you to watch, okay?

Brenda watched her mama deftly handle the knife, boring eyes out of each potato, then running the knife blade swiftly across each brown potato until it was the color of butter.

"Okay now. Mama's gonna let you try one. Take the knife. It's sharp now. You've got to be careful. Now let's tilt the blade low so it just skims the potato."

Brenda followed her mama's instructions and was confused when no skin was removed.

Viola gently laughed.

"Maybe don't tilt it quite that much," she said. "Let's try that again."

This time, Brenda went too far in the other direction. The knife pierced the skin and promptly lodged in the potato.

"That's better, but maybe a little too much Now, let's go for somewhere in between."

After several tries and her mother's patient correction, Brenda successfully removed peeling, although she took a substantial amount of potato with it.

"Good! You're doing good, Brenda! You finish that one, and I'm gonna finish these up. Then, can you get us a pot to boil these in?"

Brenda jumped down from the chair and retrieved the pot all while keeping an eye on her mama's knife skills.

Viola was a master peeler. She removed the potato skins quickly, each peel as thin as a sheet of paper and all of the potato preserved for eating.

Once the potatoes had been peeled, quartered and rinsed, Brenda, at her mama's instruction, put them in the pot she had retrieved. Viola filled the pot with water, lit an eye on the stove and set the pot over the rising heat.

"We're gonna cover the pot to help the water boil quicker," Viola told her.

Viola was careful to explain every step of a process and every reason behind a step whenever she was teaching her children. She was the reason Robert could root any cutting from flower, bush or tree and the reason Ed Earl was a good counselor to the people who attended his little church. Though she might not have realized it, Viola's patient instruction was the reason Brenda had managed to do so well in adulthood.

It didn't take long for the water to begin to roll, and 20 minutes later, the once hard potatoes were soft. Viola poured off the water, then took a fork and made quick work breaking the potatoes down. When the yellow mass had sufficiently cooled, so that Brenda wouldn't get burned, Viola handed her daughter the fork and instructed her to get rid of the lumps. She held her hand at first to show her, guiding her to find the starchy chunks and put pressure on them with the flattened fork.

Brenda mashed, looked up for her mother's approval, then mashed again, repeating that rhythm every so often, until Viola took the bowl from her

"Okay, let's get the milk, butter, salt and pepper."

When Brenda turned to retrieve the ingredients, Viola covertly completed the job of creaming the potatoes. Then, when Brenda returned, Viola set about turning what had been a mound of hard, tasteless taters into a side dish fit for any church homecoming.

She measured nothing and explained as she went.

"First let's add the butter. It needs to go in while the potatoes are still warm so that it will melt and mix in real good," Viola said. She took three heaping dinner spoons of butter and dropped them into the pot. "Keep stirring and mashing, Hon."

"Now, you don't need much milk, just enough to make the potatoes smooth and creamy, I'd say about half a cup," Viola told her as she poured the perfect amount of milk straight from the bottle.

"Now, every cook has her secret ingredient, you know?"

Brenda nodded, drinking in the experience.

"Mine is buttermilk," Viola said. "We're gonna add a little buttermilk to the potatoes now, probably about a third a cup."

To top off the side dish, Viola added salt and pepper, then took back over the mashing job, this time running the fork around the edges of the pot, then plunging it into the yellow goodness. When she felt the potatoes were sufficiently smooth, she pulled the fork out and took a taste.

"Mmmmmm them's good! You try!"

Brenda took a bite of the creamy potatoes, they warmed her mouth, then her stomach.

"Mmmmmmmmmm," Brenda repeated, trying her best to sound like her mama.

Viola covered the potatoes with a towel and set them on the kitchen table.

"We'll let them cool a while before we put in the refrigerator," she explained. "Otherwise, they'll sweat and get watery."

"We gonna cook something else?" Brenda asked.

"Well, Hon, yes, we are. I still need to cook some green beans and corn on the cob. We'll cook the turkey in the morning."

"I can help!" Brenda volunteered, and she did.

For the rest of the day Brenda learned at Viola's side. They stewed the green beans in a pot with a ham hock until they were as soft as the potatoes and no longer bright green. They shucked the corn, Viola letting Brenda pull the fine silk from between the kernels, before boiling them tender.

This time in the kitchen with mama was rare. Viola had gone back to work when Ed Earl was about two. The war was gearing up that year. Our boys were heading overseas, and the mill needed a few good women willing to work. Viola was hired right away because she was experienced. This was more time Brenda had spent with her mama than she could remember in her short life, and she wanted it to last for as long as it could.

That year, Leroy's mama, Pauline, joined them at the table. So did Shorty, a peculiar little man who lived down the street and worked at the mill with Leroy and Viola. Shorty was well past 60 and lived alone. When Viola found out he wouldn't be celebrating Thanksgiving, she invited him to join their celebration.

Viola pulled chairs from the living room and put the leaf in the table to make room for their guests. When everyone was seated, she reached out her hands to both sides. Shorty was the only one to recognize the gesture. He followed suit and took Brenda's hand in his.

Once the circle was complete, Shorty looked toward Viola.

"You reckon it'd be alright if I gave thanks?" he asked.

Viola looked at Leroy. Saying grace was not something Leroy had done regularly, but once he and Viola married, he had taken on the job just as he had taken on her faith.

"That'd be fine, Shorty," Leroy said, bowing his head.

Shorty closed his eyes and prayed.

"Lord, I sure do thank you for this here meal we're about to eat, and I thank you for the hands that prepared it, even little Brenda's. Lord, I ask you to send down your blessings on Miss Pauline, on Leroy and Viola and on these kids, because they have blessed me with the invite to join them today. Let this food strengthen our bodies to do your good work. In the name of Jesus, Amen"

"Amen!" Brenda said enthusiastically. "Can we eat now?"

Viola laughed.

Leroy looked at Brenda sternly. "Wait your turn."

"Yes sir," Brenda said meekly, dropping her chin and looking up at her father.

Soon, every plate was filled with Viola's creations.

"I helped make the potatoes and the corn and the beans," Brenda announced.

"Yes, she did," Viola said. "She was a good helper yesterday and today."

"Darlin,' you keep on helping your mama in the kitchen. That's gonna be some good skills for you one day," Shorty told her.

Shorty turned out to be a prophet. The dishes Brenda learned to make from her mama, including the turkey and her mama's apple cobbler, became holiday staples once Viola died.

After everyone had a helping of Viola's cobbler, Shorty reached into his pocket and pulled out a harmonica. He sat in a rocking chair and slowly rocked in rhythm as "Amazing Grace" rested their weary souls.

"I once was lost, but now I'm found.
Was blind, but now I see."

Shorty turned out to have other skills as well.

Robert had been scratching a wart on his index finger, and Shorty had noticed. The wart was as stubborn as a mule.

"Can I buy that wart from you?" Shorty asked.

"Sir?" Robert asked.

"I'll give you a penny for your wart," Shorty added. "Let me see your hand."

Shorty took a copper penny from his pocket, passed it over Robert's wart, then handed him the penny.

"That wart won't bother you no more."

Sure enough, the wart was gone the next day.

"You know," Shorty said to his hosts, "I can tell you about your future, too."

"Now, I don't know much about that," Viola said.

"It's okay, Miss Viola," he said. "I use a Bible and a deck of cards, and I keep both of them right here in my overalls."

Shorty retrieved a small Bible and a beat-up deck of cards from his pockets.

"Do you mind?"

"Well, if you're using God's word, I don't reckon I mind," Viola said.

Pauline and Leroy were not convinced.

Shorty divided the deck into four stacks and asked Viola to pull a card from one of the stacks.

"Four of hearts."

"Well see there," Shorty said. "That right there tells me that there are four people you love most in the world. It'd be my guess that they are all right here with us: Leroy, Robert, Brenda and Ed Earl."

"Well, would you look at that?" Viola said.

"Now, we turn to the fourth gospel, the gospel of John and read today's scripture: It's November, so that's the eleventh chapter, and today's the 26th. Let's see here."

Shorty read the verse to Viola.

"And whosoever liveth and believeth in me shall never die. Believest thou this?"

"Does that mean mama will never die?" Brenda asked.

"Well, sister, I believe what the good book says. If Miss Viola believes in our Lord, and I believe she does, then she'll live forever in heaven."

"Do mine!" Brenda said. "Do mine!"

"Well, OK, sis," Shorty said to Brenda.

He shuffled the cards, set our four stacks and repeated his instructions. Brenda pulled her card and slowly handed it to Shorty.

"I got a seven," Brenda said.

"Yes, you did, the number of completion, and you drew clubs, the symbol of the three in one. Now, we're gonna count seven books after the gospels. Let's see, that'll take us to Philippians. Now, there's not 11 chapters in that book, so we're gonna just look at today's date. Philippians 2:6 says 'Who, being in the form of God, thought it not robbery to be equal with God?'"

"Now, Brenda, my word to you is to be careful."

"Oh, I will be," Brenda said. She didn't know what she had to be careful of, but she'd sure watch out.

"You are made in the image of God, but you can't be his equal, God has no equal. You have to remember as you grow up that you can't aim to be God's equal, no siree. You're not gonna be perfect, but you are made in his image. The Good Book says so. God made you just like he wanted you, Brenda.

"As long as you remember you are made in God's image," Shorty held up the seven of clubs and pointed to each petal on the design, "and as long as you depend on the Father, the Son and the Holy Ghost, you're gonna be just fine."

Brenda didn't know what all that meant, but it made her feel good to know that she could depend on the Father, the Son AND the Holy Ghost.

"God made me in his image!" She told Robert and Ed Earl, beaming with pride in her connection to the Almighty.

"I am too!" Robert said.

"Maybe, but Shorty didn't tell you, you was. He told me I was."

Brenda skipped away. Robert stayed sitting beside his daddy. He wanted Shorty to tell him his future, too, but if his daddy wasn't going to let him open the Bible over him, he sure wasn't either. Maybe men don't do stuff like that.

"Shorty, you gonna tell Robert his future?" Brenda said, circling back through the house.

"I don't think so," Shorty said. "Robert already got his gift."

Robert looked down; his jaw dropped. Sure enough, his wart had stopped itching.

CHAPTER 22
LORDS AND LADIES

It was 9:30 in the morning, and Miss Edna and her Buick were right on time.

Brenda was waiting on the glider on the front porch. She stood and walked toward Miss Edna keeping her eyes on the ground. She opened the passenger door and took her seat, avoiding eye contact with her friend.

"Hey Miss Edna," Brenda said.

"Hey Hon, you feeling OK?"

"Yes ma'am."

Swap Shop was on the radio, and Brenda was grateful to be alone with her thoughts. *I don't know what to say. I bet Miss Edna is ashamed to be seen with me. I don't know why she even came today. I wonder what Tally, Teresa and Mae are gonna say.*

Brenda gripped her pocketbook more tightly, drawing it against her stomach. *Maybe I should just go back home.*

"This is Swap Shop, what are you gettin' rid of or what are you looking for?"

"Mike, I'm lookin' for a set of chester drawers. I need at least four drawers. It don't matter what color they are. If anybody has a set, I sure would appreciate them contacting me."

"Is it chester drawers or chest of drawers?" Miss Edna wondered out loud.

Brenda was relieved to be able to talk about something other than Knoxville, Eubanks County Hospital or Curtis Whitfield. "My mama always said chester drawers. But now that you mention it, that don't really make sense, does it?"

"I mean, I guess they could be named for somebody named Chester," Miss Edna said, hoping her joke would bring a smile to Brenda's blank face. It didn't.

"I guess so."

Swap Shop had moved on to more callers.

"I've got a small chainsaw that I'd like to get rid of, Mike."

"That's a small chainsaw. Do you have anything else you'd like to swap today?

"No sir, that'll do it."

"And what number should they call?"

The caller gave the number as Miss Edna pulled into the lot of Lords and Ladies.

Tally and the girls had been watching through the shop's big picture window for signs of Miss Edna and Brenda. The whispers had started with the first customer.

"She did what?"

"Walked from Sumner to Highway 53!"

"How far did she get?"

"Almost to the jail."

"Where did you say she was going?"

"I heard she was going to the World's Fair."

"In Knoxville?"

"Shhhh. She's comin' in!"

The beauticians and their customers scrambled back to their stations. Tally, Teresa, Mae and Earlene busied themselves with teasing combs and hairspray. Their customers thumbed through old magazines as Miss Edna and Brenda opened the door.

"Hey y'all!" Tally said, a little more animated than usual.

"Tally," Miss Edna said firmly, delivering a clear message with her greeting. She would protect her friend from the gossips, snobs and predators that waited inside the beauty shop, and she would take no prisoners in the process.

Brenda sat down, quietly waiting her turn. She kept her eyes down. This was not the typical animated Brenda whose presence in the shop usually couldn't be overlooked, and everyone knew it, including Brenda herself.

When she heard laughter, Brenda assumed it was about her. If she glanced up and caught someone's eye, she was certain they had been staring at her.

"You ready, Honey?" Teresa's voice drew her out of her thoughts and back to the moment.

Brenda walked over to the shampoo chair, leaned back and looked up at Teresa. She took a deep breath and whispered, "I almost went to the World's Fair."

"Well, Honey, that's what I heard. Why didn't you go?"

"I would've, but daddy needs me, you know. I'm the only one who cooks how he likes it, and nobody can wash his shirts the way I can. It's for the best."

"Honey, I know you work real hard taking care of your daddy and your brother, but, Sugar, everybody deserves a little vacation," Teresa said.

"I guess you wouldn't call this a vacation," Brenda replied, keeping her voice low.

The conversation continued in the styling chair.

"I was going to meet the love of my life," she whispered.

"Tell me about that, Sugar," Teresa said.

For the next few minutes, Brenda spilled out her own romanticized version of Curtis Whitfield, the Curtis she held in her mind and her heart. She told her about his unfortunate experience of being married four times to mean, selfish women and about his realization that it was Brenda herself that he had been searching for all those years.

"He was comparing every one of those women to me," Brenda said. "Can you believe it? He picked me, Brenda Lee Branch from little ol' Sumner, Georgia, over all them other girls."

Brenda told Teresa how Curtis was a hard worker, that he had had jobs in some of the biggest cities in Georgia and Tennessee and how he had worked for Delta when he lived in Peachtree City.

"And now, he's working at the World's Fair up in Knoxville," she said.

"It can't be easy to get a job at something as important as the World's Fair," she told Teresa.

"He sounds real special, Honey," Teresa said, grateful that she could think of something to say. There would be no judgment or laughter from her. She truly felt pity for her customer.

"You know," Brenda whispered, "me and Curtis would have gotten married 26 years ago, but my brother and my daddy got in the middle of it, and Curtis left. He was my first love and my first kiss. I never cared about another man."

Teresa was at a loss for advice. "Maybe the timing's just not right yet, Sugar."

Brenda sighed, then allowed her thoughts to carry her through the rest of her appointment. *My time came and went twice. I ain't so sure there will be another time.*

She sat in silence while Teresa did the only thing she knew to do. She couldn't fix Brenda's broken heart, but she could fix her hair. She teased Brenda's permed hair more vigorously than usual and took extra time to carefully lay Brenda's curls in neat rows all over her head. The poor woman deserved some kind of lift in her life, she figured, and backcombing and Aqua Net was about all she had to offer.

Brenda slid out of the styling chair and paid Teresa for her services.

"Well, we'll be praying for you, Honey," Teresa said.

"I appreciate it," Brenda said, wondering whether she really meant it.

Saying you'll pray for somebody is more platitude than religious statement at the Lords and

Ladies, and the girls all knew it. It was simply the polite thing to say, just like please and thank you.

People who say, "I'll pray for you," don't mean that they'll be on the knees for you. The statement carries the same expectation that comes with, "Let me know if there's anything I can do," at funerals and visitations. You say it because it's what you're supposed to say, not because you intend any kind of follow up. To say anything else just wouldn't be proper.

Brenda said those same words to other people, but she meant them. If she said she'd pray for you, she prayed. If she asked if there was something she could do, she didn't wait around. She cooked a casserole or sent flowers to the funeral home. And, if anyone ever sent anything to her, Leroy or Robert, she made sure not to return the dish empty. Any Southern woman worth her salt knows you don't return an empty dish. It had best have a dozen cookies or a pie in it. At a minimum, it should have a thank you note tucked inside.

Empty words, like 'I'll pray for you,' and 'Let me know if I can do anything,' especially bothered the Mullinax girls something fierce. They were part of the old guard of Southern matrons and Eastern Stars who believed a person is only as good as their word.

"A real Christian don't have to ask a family who had lost a loved one to let you know if there was anything else you could do!" Pat would say to her sister. "Of course, there's something you can do. You can cook a casserole, fry some chicken, make a dessert, or do all three and take them to the house."

If someone in Brenda's family had died, the girls at the shop would've known what to do. They would have cooked a funeral dish, secured it in Tupperware with their name written in black marker on a piece of masking tape stuck to the bottom, and delivered it to the door of Brenda's mill house. Or, they would have sent a peace lily with a card containing a Bible verse.

Some of the younger girls had started ordering fried chicken from the Piggly Wiggly deli and sending it over for funerals. Pat and Peg just couldn't stomach that idea. Sending store-bought food was just plain lazy and not at all Christian.

So, when Pat and Peg heard Teresa say she'd pray for Brenda, they looked at each other with skeptical, disapproving eyes.

"Makes my toes curl," Peg muttered to her sister-in-law. "She'd be lucky if her prayer made it out the front door."

"Shhhh," Pat replied.

Once they got into Pat's Cadillac, Peg couldn't hold herself back.

"I just don't understand it, Pat. Don't they know the Good Lord don't listen to the prayers of the sinner, unless it's the sinner's prayer? Them drinking, dancing floozies ain't got no business telling somebody they'd pray for 'em. It ain't a doin' nobody no good."

"It's just good manners," Pat replied, "That's all. Maybe you shouldn't take it to heart so much, Peg."

"Well, I don't like it. It irks me to hear them mention drinking in some bar and praying to Jesus in the same breath."

Peg believed in speaking the truth, direct and without nuance.

"The truth," she always quoted, "shall set you free."

Brenda liked people telling her they'd pray. She figured Jesus loved everybody, and she wanted all the prayers she could get.

"Your hair looks real nice, Brenda," Miss Edna said, as they settled into the car.

"Thank you, Miss Edna, yours too."

Miss Edna cranked the car and pulled onto Maple Avenue just as Paul Harvey came on the radio. He started with "*If I were the Prince of Darkness.*"

"Oh, this is a good one," Miss Edna said. The rode home in silence as they made their way down Maple.

Miss Edna parked in front of Brenda's house. Paul Harvey had finished, but Brenda wasn't aware. She had quit listening. She was thinking about the devil. *Everybody thinks Curtis is the devil, but he's not. Or maybe they think I'm the devil.*

"He's not the devil," Brenda said softly. She'd know it if he was, because Brenda was afraid of the devil, and she wasn't afraid of Curtis.

"What's that, Hon?" Miss Edna asked.

"Nothin. Thank you, Miss Edna," Brenda said.

"You're welcome."

Brenda got out of the car and headed up the sidewalk.

"Brenda?" Miss Edna leaned her head out of the window. "Everything is going to be okay."

Brenda had always been able to see the bright side of things, but this time it was hard to see any daylight at the end of this tunnel. She sure hoped Miss Edna was right.

CHAPTER 23
SMOKEY MOUNTAINS TEARS

Brenda couldn't see it, but Curtis Whitfield was the devil incarnate, Beelzebub himself, trying to disguise his darkness with light. His four ex-wives and countless ex-bosses would testify to that without coercion. But an ever-hopeful Brenda couldn't see that. She had been taken in by Curtis' swagger and stories just like the string of teenagers, tourists, college girls and waitresses who had funded his way from middle Georgia to east Tennessee.

When Brenda didn't show up in Knoxville, Curtis wasn't surprised. He was mad. He didn't like setbacks. Her failure to show meant he had to delay his trip further south until he could come up with another hustle, and he was tired of the fair life. He was getting by, and he reckoned he could make it last a few more months if he needed to, but he didn't want to.

It only took him a week to hatch his next plan.

Curtis talked his way into the World's Fair gate by hailing a golf cart driven by one of the grounds people. He faked an injury just in time for the driver to see him, earning him a free ride inside the gates and straight to the First Aid station. Once inside, he bummed a cigarette off the EMT and distracted him with one of his stories. Once clear of the medical tent, he sidled up to a girl selling cotton candy, telling her he had been stood up by the only woman he had ever loved.

"Her name was Brenda Lee, at least that's what she told me," he told her. "She told me to meet her at the World's Fair, and we would build a life together." Curtis had a good history with telling lies, and he learned a long time ago that adding a little truth to a big lie made the whole story convincing.

"But I don't think she ever intended to come here," Curtis told the vendor, dropping his head. He looked up at her with his eyes. "I had bought her a ring and everything."

The cotton candy vendor fell for his story, hook, line and sinker, and Curtis reeled her in like an expert fisherman.

"You still got the ring, don't you?" she said, talking loudly over the whirring sugar spinner. "Sell it back."

"No," he said. "I don't have the ring. I was so excited to marry her that I gave it to her early. She told me it's at the bottom of a pond."

"She threw a way a perfectly good ring?"

"And a diamond at that I tell you!" Curtis said. "She broke my heart and now I'm flat broke money-wise too. I spent my savings on the ring and my last paycheck coming up here to Knoxville."

The story worked like a charm. By the end of the day, Curtis had collected $39 and two packs of Camels. He had a good dinner with a family visiting from Canada. Then, using the quarters he swiped from the tip jar on the counter, he found a pay phone and dialed Brenda's number.

"Hello."

"Can I speak to Brenda Lee?"

"You listen to me you sorry piece of trash. Don't you ever call this house again, and if I catch you within a mile of here, me and my daddy and maybe even my preacher brother will beat you with a Louisville Slugger all the way from Sumner to Knoxville!"

Robert's face was red, his jaw set. His words were emphatic and deliberate. There was no missing the meaning. He would protect his sister at all costs.

Brenda heard it all. She wanted to grab the phone out of Robert's hand and tell Curtis she was sorry. She wanted to empty her wallet and buy a one-way Greyhound ticket to Knoxville. She wanted to tell Robert to quit being so mean and bossy, but Brenda knew she'd never do any of those things. *Why can't they see that he loves me? Why can't they see that I'm the one that messed up.* She hurried to her bedroom, laid on the bed and buried her face in her feather pillow.

  Brenda turned on the radio beside her bed. She didn't want her daddy or Robert to hear her crying. She usually kept her radio tuned to the same Southern Gospel station that her mama had favored, but all she was getting was white noise, "snow" they called it. So, she fiddled with the dial until she found an AM station playing Andy Williams.

"Oh, Danny boy, the pipes, the pipes are calling,
From glen to glen, and down the mountain side.
The summer's gone, and all the roses falling,
It's you, it's you must go and I must bide.
But come ye back when summer's in the meadow,
Or when the valley's hushed and white with snow,
I'll be here in sunshine or in shadow,
Oh, Danny boy, oh Danny boy, I love you so!
But when ye come, and all the flowers are dying,
If I am dead, as dead I well may be,
You'll come and find the place where I am lying,
And kneel and say an Ave there for me.

And I shall hear, though soft you tread above me,
And all my grave will warmer, sweeter be,

For you will bend and tell me that you love me,
And I shall sleep in peace until you come to me!"

Robert Branch's one-sided conversation redirected Curtis. He was done with Knoxville. So, he called Brenda to test the waters for a trip Sumner. Now he knew he'd better steer clear of Eubanks County. He thought about heading to Nashville, but it was summertime, and it would be full of hustlers like him. He didn't like that much competition. So, he headed back toward the Smokies, thumbing a ride with a semi-truck to Pigeon Forge.

It was midnight when Curtis jumped out of the truck. The little town was beginning to wind down. He stepped into the Waffle House, hoping to snare a cup of coffee and a waitress, and he did.

Her name was Ruthie Johnson, and she was working at the 24-hour breakfast restaurant until she could save enough money for a car. Once she bought a car—she didn't care what kind it was—Ruthie was going to drive as far away from the mountain town as she could. She was getting close. Ruthie had nearly $500, and she figured she could get a used Chevette or Pinto for $750.

Ruthie kept pouring Curtis coffee, and Curtis kept Ruthie talking. He told her he had a Vietnam injury that had cost him his job and that Robert Branch had forbid him from ever seeing the love of his life again. Curtis told Ruthie he was like her, just trying to get out of the mountains, and back somewhere where people were decent and would give a guy who couldn't hardly work a chance. Ruthie invited him home with her.

Curtis woke up early and snuck out the door in his bare feet. He sat down on the front steps to put his boots on, walked to the end of the street and thumbed a ride up the mountain to Gatlinburg. He had $542 in his pocket. Ruthie would be working a whole lot longer to get out of the Smokies.

CHAPTER 24
SUNDAY MORNING SERVICE

The phone rang about 7 o'clock. Brenda was already up, making coffee and cooking the expected Sunday morning breakfast.

"Hello."

Her sister-in-law, Mary Jo, was on the line.

"Yes, I plan to go to church this morning. I'll be ready as soon as I'm done with breakfast. Okay. Bye now."

She retrieved the cast iron skillet and dropped the fatback into it. She turned on the stove eye and let the gas heat cook the pork until it had curled up and begun to char. Brenda tore a couple of paper towels off, folded them and laid them across a plate, then removed the skillet from the heat and deposited the strips of salty pork onto the paper, allowing the towels to soak up the remaining grease. With the skillet sufficiently cooled, she added the sausage patties, allowing the grease from the fatback to mingle with the sage-heavy sausage.

There was an order to cooking a proper breakfast that she had taken pride in before her decision to meet up with Curtis. She would put on her mama's apron and follow the steps that she had been taught years ago. The grease from the fatback and sausage made a perfect seasoning for the hen eggs that she then added to the deep skillet. *Watch the eggs, Brenda. You can't let the yolks set.* Once the whites had set a little, Brenda used the spatula to rake the pork grease over the yolks. Her daddy and brother liked their eggs sunny side up with the whites browned around the edges. Cooking the eggs in the sausage and fat back grease added plenty of flavoring, but Leroy and Robert always added salt and black pepper to their eggs after they were on the plate.

Buttermilk biscuits, made from scratch the way Viola had taught her daughter, were browning in the oven. They weren't the thick fluffy biscuits a lot of families had. Her mama had always kept them flat and a little crunchy, concentrating the taste into a smaller bite. The flat biscuits had started as a mistake. Viola had used warm butter and overmixed the dough. She was ready to throw the thin, crunchy biscuits away and start over, but Leroy had grabbed one and stuffed it into his mouth. He bragged on the flat bread so much that Viola made them that way from then on.

Brenda never knew there was another way to make them, and she took pride in cutting the biscuits from the same tin can opened on both ends that her mama had used. Brenda always made 2 dozen biscuits at a time. Eight of them were eaten at breakfast. The rest served as the bread for lunch and dinner. Then, if there was any left, the remaining biscuits made a fine dessert at the end of the day. She loved taking one of the flat biscuits out, cutting it open, adding a pat of butter to the middle, then heating it up in the oven. Once the biscuit was warm and the butter was melted, Brenda would spoon sugar into the center, on top of the butter, then place the top back onto the buttered and sugared bottom. Eaten with a glass of cold sweet milk, it was as good as any wedding cake or groom's cake she had ever eaten.

After cleaning up from breakfast, Brenda quickly finished getting ready for Sunday School.

Brenda had gone to Sunday School for as long as she could remember. When she was a girl, she liked the felt board stories of Jesus walking on the water or Daniel in the lion's den. Sometimes she wished they'd use those felt boards for the adult lessons. The whole armor of God would be a whole lot more interesting if you could add the breastplate of righteousness to a felt

Paul. Instead, the class took turns reading paragraphs out of the quarterly. Luckily, Brenda was a decent reader. That was not true of everybody in the class, and in her current state, Brenda had to clinch her teeth when the teacher called on a poor reader.

She wouldn't dare complain or make fun like Curtis had of stuttering Ben, but today she sure did wish they could skip the people who had a hard time reading. It made the lesson take twice as long, it was embarrassing to both the reader and the listeners and, today, it was gettin' on her last nerve.

"Put ... on the ... whole ... ar- armour of God... that ... ye ...may be ... able ... to stand ... against ... against the ... the ... the ... wiles of the devil.

"For ... we ... wor ... wer ... reh ... wrestle not ... against ... flesh ... and ... blood, but ... against ... against ..."

Bless his heart. He ain't ever gonna get through this.

"Lord, help him," she prayed to herself. "Tell somebody to say the word for him."

"Puh ... puh ... pre ... prin ... prink ... principal ..."

"Jesus, please loosen his tongue," Brenda said, mouthing the words as she prayed.

"Principalities ..."

Hallelujah! He got it! Brenda was ashamed that she was feeling this way, but powerless over how she felt in the moment.

"... against ... powers ... against the ... rulers ... of the ... darkness of ... this world, ... against ... sp ... spirit ... spiritual ... wickedness."

Whoop! Praise the Lord, he got wickedness on first try! Brenda kept her thoughts to herself, surprised at her own wicked reaction to the slow reader.

After the Sunday School offering and the prayer requests, Brenda pulled her purse close in and walked, head down, to the sanctuary.

Her usual spot was on the third row on the aisle. She liked to be able to see her brother preach, but she didn't want to be right up front in case people started shoutin' or fallin' out in the Spirit. They were Baptist, but that didn't mean the Spirit didn't move.

After everyone shook hands and said, "Hey," to each other, the song leader came out and told everybody to join him. Let's sing *Victory in Jesus!*

"*I heard an old, old story.*
How a savior came from glory.
How me made the lame
To walk again,
And He caused the blind to see."

Brenda sang quietly at first but gained confidence—and volume—as the song headed to the chorus.

"Oh, victory in Jesus," Brenda sang a little too loudly.

"My savior forever.
"He sought me, and He bought me
"With His redeeming blood.
"He loved me e'er I knew Him," her voice cracked at the high notes.

"And all my love is due Him.
"He plunged me to VICTORY!
"Beneath the cleansing flood," Brenda tried a little harmony at the end. It didn't go so well, but nobody seemed to mind.

The song ended, and before they could start the next one, a shaky voice rose from the back, above the crowd.

"I'd like to stand and say I love the Lord."

It was Sister Delia, she started crying as soon as she stood up. She was a short lady, not even 5-feet tall, but the extra foot of hair on top of her head made her appear taller. "The Lord has been so good to me. He saved my soul. He's took care of me and my family. We've got a shelter over our heads and shoes on our feet. He's give me a good man who works hard and loves his family..."

Tears begin to trickle down Brenda's face. She was glad for Sister Delia, and she was glad that she understood what a blessing it was to have a good man in your life, a man who loved you and took care of you.

Brenda gripped the back of the pew in front of her, hard. She knew all her love was due to Jesus, but was it bad for her to want a man to love her, a man like Sister Delia had? Her daddy had loved her mama. Couldn't she have that with Curtis?

"I once was lost in sin,
But Jesus took me in.
And, then a little light from heaven
Filled my soul.
He filled my heart with love,
And wrote my name above.
And just a little talk with Jesus
Made me whole."

Brenda knew she needed to talk to the Lord, but she didn't know what to say. Should she ask for forgiveness or for Curtis? Should she ask for the Lord to help Robert and her daddy understand how she felt, or should she ask for a change of heart?

The last thought scared her. What if Jesus took away her love for Curtis? Who would take care of him? *I'd never love anyone again.*

She made it through the song service without going up to the altar for prayer, and she was glad when it was time to sit down.

Ed Earl walked behind the pulpit and looked straight at her.

"Greater love hath no man than this," Ed Earl quoted, "that a man lay down his life for his friends."

"AMEN!"

"HALLELUJAH!"

Ed Earl started slow.

"Brothers and sisters, people do not know love. Oh, they say they do, but they don't. They use it, abuse it and lose it, but they don't know it. I'm tellin' you this morning, love is a word that has been thrown around so much that it's lost its meaning, and that is damaging the gospel of Jesus Christ."

"Amen, brother!"

"When you can love a dog, fried chicken, your car, your wife *and* the good Lord, that's a problem right there. How can you use the same word, hah, to describe, hah, how you feel about chicken, hah, as you do about Jesus, hah. It ain't right, hah, it ain't good, hah, and it ain't love, hah!"

"Preach it, preacher!"

"Look here what the word of God says about love. Turn in your Bibles to Romans, chapter 8. Brother Paul says right here in verse 35, 'Who shall separate us from the love of Christ? Shall tribulation, or distress, or persecution, or famine, or nakedness, or peril or sword?' Then, in verse 37, he says Nay! That means No!

"If all it takes is a little trouble, a little distress, going hungry or not having fine clothes to make you turn away from the Lord, you didn't love Him, not like you should."

Brenda didn't feel like she had turned away from the Lord. She had just turned toward Curtis Whitfield. Did it have to be one or the other? Couldn't she love both of them?

"In the book of Revelation, hah, the good Lord says, hah, I have THIS against you, hah. You have left your first love. Won't you come back to Him?"

The song leader had returned to the front of the church.

"Oh, what peace we often forfeit.
Oh, what needless pain we bear.
All because we do not carry
Everything to God in prayer."

Brenda and the rest of the congregation were standing, and she was again holding on to the back of the pew. She was crying, but not, she realized, because she had left her first love. No, these tears were for her lost opportunity, her fading memories and a life with Curtis that she would never know.

CHAPTER 25
INDEPENDENCE DAY

The Fourth of July was Sunday, and for the first time since she had gotten out of the hospital, Brenda felt a twinge of excitement.

When she and Miss Edna got to the beauty shop on the third, the girls were more animated than usual. Jane Ellen had spent the night out honky-tonking and had the whole shop laughing at her story of a wannabe cowboy who tried to impress her with his line-dancing skills, only to wind up with a split in his jeans and a bruised ego.

"I tell you one thing, he wasn't no cowboy, urban or otherwise," Jane Ellen said.

The entire shop cackled with laughter. When the conversation turned to plans for the Fourth, Earlene said she was making homemade chocolate ice cream.

You just had to know Earlene. Like Brenda, she carried an air of innocence. She was as sweet as the day was long, but every once in a while, she would say something so off the wall that even Brenda was left scratching her head.

"My friend told me to go over to the college and get some of their chocolate milk to make my chocolate ice cream," Earlene said.

Miss Edna spoke up.

"Earlene, Hon, you don't have to have chocolate milk to make chocolate ice cream. You just add some cocoa to the recipe."

"Oh no ma'am," Earlene said. "Bobby told me to go over to the dairy at the college and ask for some of the chocolate milk that comes from their brown cows."

The Lords and Ladies Beauty Shop erupted into laughter.

"Why y'all laughin'?" Earlene asked with the sincerity of a nun. "Bobby said they have a whole herd of brown dairy cows that give chocolate milk."

"Earlene, bless your heart," Teresa said, tears of laughter streaming mascara down her face. "Are you saying you think sweet milk comes only from white cows?"

"Well, those black and white ones make the sweet milk too," Earlene said.

Laughter erupted again.

"Hon," Miss Edna said, "Bobby was pullin' your leg. Ain't no brown cow ever give chocolate milk. That's like sayin' it takes a blue chicken to lay Easter eggs."

The look of confusion on Earlene's face was priceless.

"How in land's sake could she grow up this close to the country and not know that cows don't give chocolate milk?" Pat said to Peg, making no attempt to lower her voice.

"Peg, do you remember that city boy who tried to get a date with a girl from South Georgia?" Pat asked her sister-in-law. "That little sorority girl told him that her daddy owned a grits plantation. A GRITS PLANTATION! That feller went home telling his mama and daddy all about the grits trees in the South. Darlin,' if corn stalks get as big as trees, we're all gonna start living on plantations!"

The beauty shop girls howled again.

The laughter was good medicine all around, even if it had come at Earlene's expense. When Teresa had finished with Brenda and Tally with Miss Edna, they weren't in any hurry to leave, but there were preparations that needed to be made. Independence Day in Sumner was about as big as the West Oaks homecoming or Christmas at First Baptist.

Brenda and Miss Edna scooted out and headed toward the Piggly Wiggly. Miss Edna needed a watermelon, and Brenda was happy to go along for the ride. Brenda, Leroy and Robert didn't do anything special for the Fourth. Brenda would walk up the street to watch the Sumner Fourth of July parade, but that wasn't enough of a celebration in her mind. She'd always thought it would be nice to hang a flag on their porch post or to paint some tires red, white and blue and plant flowers in them. A lot of folks did that back in '76 for the bicentennial. Shoot, even the fire department painted the fire hydrants with stars and stripes. Brenda wanted to do *something* more than just see the parade. Maybe she could get a small watermelon or a half-gallon of ice cream. Besides, a half-hour at the Piggly Wiggly was 30 minutes less that she had to spend at home with Robert. There had been an uneasy tension between Brenda and her older brother since her return from the hospital, and Robert's warning to Curtis had made it worse. It would pass like it always did, but for now, it was best for them to limit their time together, she figured.

Brenda walked up and down the aisles with Miss Edna. Since she didn't need anything, she just scanned the shelves for inspiration. When they got to the cookies, Brenda got some Oreos, and further down, she picked up a bag of Ruffles. She liked to take

Ruffles in her lunch, and the Oreos just looked like they'd taste good with a big ol' glass of sweet milk. That thought made her laugh out loud.

"Can you believe Earlene thought chocolate milk came from brown cows?" Brenda said to Miss Edna.

Both women started laughing again.

"Can you imagine if that girl had gone up to the college to ask for chocolate milk?" Miss Edna said. "Honestly, if Earlene Thompson had a brain, she'd never go to sleep for fear she'd lose it during the night."

After they paid for their groceries, Miss Edna and Brenda got back in the car for the short drive home. A baseball game was on the radio station they normally listened to, so Miss Edna began punching buttons, looking for some entertainment.

"Grilling fruit brings out its sweetness," the man on the radio said.

"Grilling fruit! Have you ever heard such a thing?" Miss Edna wondered aloud. "Do you reckon they eat it hot? I just can't even tolerate that idea."

"Most every fruit is suitable for grilling," the man said. "I particularly like larger, firm fruits like pineapple and cantaloupe, but watermelon, peaches and even strawberries are excellent on the grill. The addition of heat, particularly direct heat from flames, caramelizes the natural sugar in the fruit."

"I mean, it's different if it's in a pie," Miss Edna continued, "but if it's right off the grill like a hamburger, I don't know. I just ain't never heard such a thing."

The man on the radio added a twist to his grilling idea that about sent Miss Edna over the edge.

"Did he just say to put grilled pineapple on top of a hamburger patty?" Miss Edna asked Brenda. "Have you ever?"

She clicked off the radio.

"Well, I remember my mama baking apples on top of pork chops, and I remember seeing a recipe in *Southern Living* where they put pineapples and cherries on ham. Maybe a slice of pineapple on a hamburger ain't such a bad idea," Brenda said.

"Would Leroy or your brother eat it?" Miss Edna asked.

Brenda laughed. "No, they wouldn't."

"Well, there you go. Mine wouldn't either," Miss Edna said. "That settles it. Ain't nobody puttin' no grilled fruit on any burger at my house anytime soon."

As they neared Avenue D, Miss Edna broached the subject of Brenda's recovery.

"Brenda, you seem to be feelin' better, are things looking up for you, Baby?"

"They are," Brenda said. "I think they gave me something in the hospital that made me kind of groggy for a while. Now that the medicine is wearing off, I'm beginning to feel more like myself."

"That's good. That's real good. Is there anything I can do for you?" Miss Edna asked.

"I don't think so," Brenda said. "Ed Earl's church helped daddy and Robert with meals while I was gone. We don't need any groceries, and I've got food for lunches next week."

Miss Edna pulled up outside Brenda's house.

"You gonna watch the parade ain't you?" Miss Edna called out as Brenda walked toward the front door.

"I think I might," Brenda said. "We'll see."

The Sumner Fourth of July parade was a hometown tradition that started back during World War II. That year, with several hometown boys fighting overseas, the people of Sumner felt like they needed to do something to honor their service. Usually, people would go to Paris for their big celebration, but that July 4, the citizens of Sumner put together a parade of bicycles, wagons, horses and marchers to fly the red, white and blue. A brass band played a couple of hastily put together patriotic songs, and the volunteer firemen added their bright red truck to the procession. It was a sight to see.

More than forty years later, the parade hadn't changed much. The brass band has been replaced by the entire West Oaks High marching band. Cheerleaders from the high school, middle school and elementary school joined in. They marched and cheered or sat on the backs of flat-bed trucks decorated with flags and streamers. Little ones still pulled their dogs in their Radio Flyers. Boys and girls decorated their bicycles and rode them in circles. The West Oaks homecoming queen sat in the back of convertible, her name carefully drawn in glue on white poster board, then sprinkled with red and blue glitter. The best addition to the parade was the veterans, dressed in their uniforms. They marched in formation, carrying the stars and stripes. It felt like the whole town saluted when they passed by, even those not standing at the road.

Brenda couldn't help but feel the excitement of the holiday. After church, where Brother Alan had led everybody to sing *Glory, Glory Hallelujah* and *God Bless America,* Brenda came home, changed clothes and cooked a big spread. Sunday had its expected menu just like the other days, and the expected menu didn't change just because it was a holiday. The Sunday meal required a little extra preparation on

Saturday, but Brenda didn't mind. The day before, she cooked potatoes and made potato salad with mayonnaise, yellow mustard, boiled eggs, pickle relish, fine-chopped onions and paprika. Potato salad was always better when it sat overnight. Sunday after church, Brenda fried chicken and fixed a good helping of green beans.

After she, Leroy and Robert ate dinner, Brenda walked up the street to stand with her neighbors along Maple Avenue. July in Sumner announced the holiday even without the parade. Crape myrtles looked like exploding fireworks in purple, pink and white, and several of the mill houses flew American flags from porch columns.

Brenda could hear the drummers and turned in that direction to see who was coming first. It looked like the football team. They were in their uniforms on the back of a truck with red, white and blue bunting on each side. They boys were throwing candy at the crowd on both sides of the road. One of them winked in Brenda's direction. She blushed, and before she knew it, she was thinking about Curtis and the first time she had met him back in 1955.

She didn't know how long it would take for her to quit thinking about Curtis. It had been almost a month since she had set out for Knoxville. Maybe she never would stop thinking about him.

Brenda could hear her mama's voice reminding her, "These things take time." Time was all she had.

CHAPTER 26
THE BRANCH FAMILY SECRET

Exactly three people in Sumner, Georgia knew that Brenda had had electroshock therapy, and the three of them swore they would never tell a living soul about it. They had kept the secret for nearly 20 years, and that wasn't going to change. Ed Earl, Robert and Leroy would go to their graves with that information.

Viola Branch had not been feeling well for some time. It started a couple of years after Brenda graduated from high school, and gradually took her to bed. Her decline was slow, but steady and unrelenting. She went to a doctor, who prescribed diet changes and blood pressure medicine, but Viola abandoned both when they didn't make a difference in how she felt.

When making a bed or walking to the mailbox became impossible chores, her family tried to get her to go back to the doctor, but Viola would have nothing of it. The doctor had been wrong before. Why would she trust one now?

Leroy, Robert, Ed Earl and Brenda took turns taking care of Viola the last two years of her life. They volunteered for second- and third- shifts at the mill so one of them would always be with her. The Branches couldn't afford a nurse to stay at the house with her, but they wouldn't have hired one anyway, even if they could. Viola had nursed her family through flus, whooping cough, mumps, chicken pox, stomach aches, strep throat and more, now it was their turn. Neighbors would stay with Viola from time to time, and church folks helped too, bringing meals to the house and running errands. Most days, though, it was either Leroy, Robert, Ed Earl or Brenda at her side.

Viola held on through Christmas of 1964. That year, the family moved her hospital bed into the living room so she could see the Christmas tree. They ate Christmas dinner around her bed.

That Christmas was the first time Brenda was solely responsible for a holiday meal. She had helped her mama before, but she had never baked a ham by herself, and it just didn't feel right for her to be trying to replicate her mama's signature sweet potato casserole. As bad as she hated to admit it, Brenda walked in fear that this could be her mama's last Christmas, so she *had* to try. Some parts of the meal were a cinch. The cranberry sauce was easy. The Branches preferred theirs out of the can. She knew the basics of cooking dinner rolls from scratch, and creamed corn and green beans were easy enough. The chess pie worried her a little bit, but she succeeded there too. It helped that her mama was watching from the living room and still able to give a little direction.

"A teaspoon of salt, Mama?" Viola shook her head.

"Half a teaspoon then." Her mama nodded.

With her mama's guidance, Brenda cooked a fitting Christmas spread. The meal itself was eaten mostly in silence. Ed Earl complimented her efforts while Leroy spoon-fed Viola tiny bites of corn, cranberry sauce and casserole. Viola nodded her approval.

The Branch matriarch knew her time had come, but she refused to give up the ghost. She would not ruin Christmas for her family. So, she willed herself to live through Christmas Day. But as December gave way to January, it was clear that Viola's journey was nearing its end. Leroy and the boys were at work when Viola's breathing became labored. Brenda went straight to her mama's side and held her hand.

"Brenda, Hon?"

"Yes ma'am."

"I'm gonna have to go."

"No, mama. Please don't leave us," Brenda said, tears streaming down her face.

"It's time. I can see the angels. They're here for me."

"Please don't go, mama. We can't make it without you."

"Brenda, you're a strong, smart girl." Viola paused to get her breath. "Your daddy and your brothers need you. You're gonna have to be the woman of the house."

Viola stopped to take a few more shallow breaths.

"I want you to get my yellow apron, the one with the pretty pink flowers on it, and wear it every time you cook. You'll remember everything you learned from me in the kitchen, and everything will be OK. Now, go on and get that apron."

Ever obedient, Brenda went to the drawer in the kitchen where her mama kept her aprons and hand towels.

When she came back to her mama's bedside wearing the yellow apron, Viola was gone.

The realization that she had not been there, holding her mama's hand for her last breath on earth caused something to snap in Brenda's brain.

She didn't cry. She didn't scream. She sat in the chair beside her mama's bed, took her hand and held it, staring stoically ahead.

The sun set, but Brenda didn't move. Her stomach growled, but she didn't cook supper. The house grew dark, but she didn't turn on any lights. Brenda didn't go to the bathroom. She didn't get anything to drink. She just sat beside her mama staring blankly toward the kitchen.

Ed Earl was the first to arrive home. The house was completely dark. The only sound was the kitchen radio.

"When peace like a river, attendeth my way,
When sorrows like sea billows roll
Whatever my lot, thou hast taught me to say
It is well, it is well, with my soul
"It is well
With my soul
It is well, it is well with my soul
"Though Satan should buffet, though trials should come,
Let this blest assurance control,
That Christ has regarded my helpless estate,
And hath shed His own blood for my soul
"It is well
With my soul
It is well, it is well with my soul."

Ed Earl turned on the overhead light, took Viola's now-cold hand in his and knew that she was gone.

He moved to the other side of the bed and touched Brenda on the shoulder.

"Brenda, Honey. She's gone. You've got to let go of mama's hand."

Brenda didn't move, nor did she speak.

Ed Earl called the mill to tell them to tell his daddy and his brother to come home.

He called the funeral home and asked them to come, and he called the preacher and told him the news.

As the house filled with people, the noise levels rose, but Brenda said nothing and never left her chair.

"Honey, don't you need something to eat?" a church member asked.

Brenda didn't reply.

"Sister Brenda, yer mama's gone to be with the Lord. Let's let the mortician get her ready for the funeral."

Brenda didn't move.

"Miss Branch? I know this is hard, but we're gonna have to take your mama to the funeral home," a young fellow with slicked-back hair said. He was dressed in black pants, a white shirt and a tie that looked like it belonged on a grocery store clerk.

Brenda didn't respond.

Finally, Leroy took Brenda's hand in one of his hands and Viola's hand in the other. He forced their hands apart. Brenda's emotions erupted in a sob that she could not control. All conversation stopped.

She screamed a long cry of anguish, then gasped until she was unable to take any more oxygen in. This was followed by a big exhale and a series of short, stuttered breaths. She repeated this cycle of screams and tears for the next six hours, never eating, never speaking. She was lost in a canyon of grief.

Brenda's sobs didn't stop until Ed Earl got her to Eubanks County Hospital. He explained to the nurse what had happened.

"She's in shock, Honey," the nurse said.

"Miss Branch, I'm gonna take you back here and help you, okay?"

Brenda said nothing.

Brenda spent the next five days in the hospital. They had given her Valium, and that allowed her to rest, but as soon as the drug wore off, she returned to her irregular breathing and deep sobs. She could not talk. She could not move, not even to go to the bathroom. She was locked in her own thoughts, unable to communicate, unable to express her grief.

Brenda missed her mother's visitation at the funeral home. She missed the funeral, and she missed the graveside service. A few people at the funeral home asked about her, but most people knew. Sumner was a small town, and news of a nervous breakdown had its way of running through town faster than Silver Creek in wet weather. It just didn't feel right not to ask. Her daddy, Ed Earl and Robert stood by the casket, accepting hugs and handshakes. Ed Earl answered the questions as best he could. It was the three of them on the front row of the church for the service and the three of them sitting at the gravesite, forced to look into the dark hole that was to be Viola's final resting place.

"O death, where is thy sting? O grave, where is thy victory?"

The preacher's words rang hollow for Leroy and Robert. *I'll tell you where it is,* Leroy thought to himself. *It's right here in this hole.* Leroy didn't cry that day. He reserved his tears for the night, but he, too, was broken.

Brenda had been suspended in her shock for three days when her doctor told her daddy she would need something more invasive to help her. They would apply an electric shock to her brain. It would bring her out of her shock, and she likely would not remember the episode at all.

Leroy nodded his approval and went and sat in his car. *How am I supposed to make these kinds of decisions without Viola? What are you doing, Lord, taking away my wife and causing my daughter to go crazy? Is she gonna be a vegetable that I have to take care of the rest of my life without Viola? I can't do that. People always say the Lord won't put any more on you than you can bear, but, dang it, this seems like more than any one man can handle.* Leroy gripped the steering wheel until his knuckles were white and his arms trembled. That was the day Leroy quit praying.

On Jan. 29, 1965, technicians connected a series of electrodes to Brenda's head. Within a few minutes, the month of January was effectively erased from her memory. When she woke up, she was calm, groggy, and confused. After she showed signs that she was stable, Brenda was allowed to go home with a month of her life forever gone.

CHAPTER 27
ORDER OF THE EASTERN STAR, 1965

Viola Branch's faith was legendary in Sumner. She had long been a member of the Order of the Eastern Star, and everyone who knew her knew that she deserved to be associated with the Fairest of Ten Thousand and was altogether lovely. So, it was fitting that the Sisters in the Order delivered their solemn rights at her funeral.

Ed Earl, who had already announced his call, preached his mama's going home celebration. Leroy and Robert looked lost sitting on the family pew. Brenda's absence was noticeable and, of course, the chatter had started before the pallbearers entered the church.

"Brenda ain't here."

"Shhhh. I know. I heard she's still in the hospital. Bless her heart."

"Does anybody know what's wrong with her?"

"She kindly had a nervous breakdown."

"That girl loved her mama."

"Yes, she did. It's a shame she ain't here to see her mama laid to rest."

"Ain't it?"

The piano started just as the pallbearers entered from the back of the church.

"What a fellowship, what a joy divine,
Leaning on the Everlasting Arms.
What a blessedness, what a peace is mine,
Leaning on the Everlasting Arms.
Leaning,"

"On Jesus," you could hear whispered responses to the song across the congregation.

"Leaning,"

"On Jesus."

"Safe and secure from all alarms;
Leaning,"

"On Jesus."

"Leaning,"

"On Jesus."

"Leaning on the Everlasting Arms."

Sister Martha skipped the second verse.

"What have I to dread, what have I to fear,
Leaning on the Everlasting Arms.

I have peace complete with my Lord so near,
Leaning on the Everlasting Arms."

Leroy had heard that song sung a hundred times, but today, he didn't much feel like leaning. He wasn't dreading or fearing. He was empty, just empty. Without Viola, Leroy was lost.

After Ed Earl said his piece, the Eastern Star sisters came to the front. Dressed in white, as their ritual required, the sisters choked back tears as they read from their handbook.

"Sisters and Brothers, we have gathered at this solemn hour to perform those final rites which affection has prescribed for our departed sister. She, who was with us but yesterday, has been summoned hence by a messenger who cometh sooner or later for us all.

"How appropriately may we gather around her remains and together pay love's tribute to her memory.

"She has indeed passed beyond the reach of praise or the touch of censure. It is not, therefore, to her that we tender this, our heart's saddest offering."

If it hadn't been a funeral, the ritual might have drawn a chuckle from Sumner's more educated folk. The Eastern Star sisters spoke in the same country drawl as they did when they spoke on their party-line phones. The sixty-four-dollar, poetic words of their ritual would have been out of place on any other day, but the sisters revere the Order of the Eastern Star. They spoke the words exactly as they were written.

"Our sister has finished her allotted task in the conflict of life. The chapter of her earthly sojourn is closed, but her many virtues shall not go unrecorded.

"For a time, we have walked with her in the pilgrimage of life, and around the same altar we have learned the lessons of our Order.

"As she was faithful to her convictions of right, as she was obedient to the demands of honor and justice in her station; as she loved kindred and friends and in affliction evinced a trustful faith; and as she lived in the spirit of charity and the love of truth, so shall be her reward.

"Remembering her many virtues, we are indeed mourners at her grave and in the house of sorrow we would drop the tear of affectionate sympathy."

The Sisters continued to read, reminding the mourners of the brevity of life and the hope of a reward of a mansion in heaven. After a song, the sisters delivered their flower ceremony.

Assisted by one of the funeral directors, a white-dressed woman stepped up to the podium. She wiped her eyes, took a deep breath and began.

"Blue symbolizes Fidelity and is appropriate to Jephthah's Daughter, who, in the morning of life, surrendered to the grave the brightest of earthly hopes, that she might be faithful to her convictions of right and preserve her father's honor. As a token of faithfulness to the memory of our sister, I deposit this tribute of faithful love."

A similarly dressed sister followed.

"Yellow symbolizes Constancy, teaching faithful obedience to the demands of honor and justice. Ruth exemplified these virtues in humble station and sought the society of the good and true. In token of appreciation of these virtues, I deposit this floral tribute."

The third sister held up a white flower.

"White symbolizes Light and Purity. White evinces her purity of motive and love of kindred and friends by her willingness to risk the loss of crown and life, to save her people from death. In token of sincere affection for our sister, I deposit this emblem of Light and Purity."

The next sister selected a sprig of cedar and read from the book.

"Green is an emblem of nature's life and beauty. The evergreen is a symbol of Immortal Life and teaches us that in the economy of God, there is no death; forms change, but the spirit survives. Martha, beside the grave of her beloved brother, avowed her trustful faith and hope of immortal life. In the full assurance of our sister's entrance upon a glorious immortality, I deposit this evergreen."

Imogene Sutton, who had been Viola's closest friend, delivered the fifth, and final, color. She could hardly be understood through her tears.

"Red symbolizes Fervency and Zeal," she said, her voice trembling. "Red represents those who have been pre-eminent in charity and heroic in endurance of the wrongs of persecution."

Imogene's voice trailed off on persecution, making it barely audible, but no one minded. Viola was a matriarch and a loyal friend. Such emotion displayed in her honor were part of the tribute.

"In token of the fervency of our affection for our sister, I deposit this tribute of love."

Imogene braved through her emotions, even as she said her final goodbye to her friend.

The Worthy Matron finished the ritual.

"These beautiful flowers are the highest expression of nature's loveliness. We never tire of looking at their perfect and delicately variegated tints. From time immemorial, they have been endowed with expressive language. They speak to us, to whisper hope whene'er our faith grows dim. But these floral emblems, with all their exquisite loveliness, are but dim reflections of the glories that may be unfolded to our spiritual vision."

The service ended with a prayer, led by Ed Earl, and a harmonious three verses of "Amazing Grace," ending with the hopeful last verse.

> *"When we've been there*
> *Ten-thousand years,*
> *Bright shining as the sun.*
> *We've no less days.*
> *To sing God's praise,*
> *Then when we first begun."*

The hour-long service ended with family and friends filing single file by Viola's open coffin, giving each mourner one last opportunity to say good-bye.

From there, friends, family and church members made their way to their cars and trucks and drove slowly to the cemetery, their headlights on to signal they were part of the funeral procession.

Leroy and Robert endured the spectacle of the motorcade as it crept through Sumner. Cars pulled to the shoulder or stopped in the middle of the lane as a show of respect for the departed. It didn't matter whether the drivers knew the person in the hearse or not; it's what you do in the South.

At the graveyard, the six pallbearers hoisted Viola's pearlescent pink casket from the back of the hearse, then carried it the 100 or so yards to a green tent with two rows of velvet-covered folding chairs lined parallel to a dark rectangular hole. Somebody from the funeral home had lined the sides of the hole in green indoor/outdoor carpet. Brass poles formed a fence around the hole. The horizontal poles supported straps a grave closer would use to gently lower Viola into the Georgia red clay.

Ed Earl said a few words about the Lord's resurrection. As he finished, Sister Martha and Sister Jean sang "I'll Fly Away" in the prettiest harmony you could imagine.

"When I die, hallelujah by and by,
I'll fly away."

A prayer closed out the graveside service. Then Ed Earl, followed by the deacons, the pallbearers and funeral home staff, made their way down the front row of chairs, shaking hands with Leroy and Robert and the Eastern Star matrons.

"I'm sorry for your loss."

"We'll be prayin' for you."

"She's in a better place now."

"Y'all let us know if we can do anything for you."

"I'll be by later to pick up the wreath and podium from the house."

The last voice was Paul, who had run the Sumner funeral home for as long as anybody could remember. Leroy had forgotten about the wreath on their front gate. It was pure white and made of silk flowers that never faded. A brown wooden podium had been set up just inside the Branch's front door so that visitors could sign it. Leroy wouldn't miss the podium. He had slammed his toe into it no less than three times. He didn't much care for the wreath either.

"Feels like you're advertising that somebody died," he had told Robert. "I don't like it. I don't want nobody's pity, and I don't want every car on the street slowing down in front of our house."

"Well, daddy, it's just what people do when there's a death in the family, you know," Robert had answered.

"Well, I still don't like it," Leroy had countered.

At the cemetery, friends and family made sure to hug and shake hands, unaware that the staff was gently leading them away from the tent that covered Viola's grave. The funeral home staff was ready to move on. With the family and the matrons all in their cars and safely out of sight, the crew lowered Viola into the ground and made quick work of filling the hole and mounding the dirt that would eventually settle into a flat, pristine lawn.

Back home, Leroy, Robert and Ed Earl ate fried chicken and potato salad that Ed Earl's wife had served on Chinet plates. They ate in silence, the house quiet, except for Mary Jo's movement in the kitchen and Viola's radio dispatching "When I Wake Up to Sleep No More."

CHAPTER 28
MAMA'S YELLOW APRON, 1965

Brenda shuffled into the house. It was eerily quiet and felt empty.

"Mama?" she said in a small, shaky voice. "Mama?"

Ed Earl reached out and touched Brenda's elbow.

"Brenda, Honey, mama ain't here."

"Where did she go?" Brenda's voice sounded innocent, almost childlike.

Leroy and Robert left it to Ed Earl to set her straight.

"Sugar, mama died."

"She died?" Brenda asked. Her eyes filled with tears. "When did she die?"

"Brenda, Honey, you've been real sick. She died last week."

"When's the funeral?"

"Darlin,' they's already been a funeral when you was in the hospital."

"I didn't get to say goodbye," Brenda said, tears now streaming. "I didn't get to tell her I love her."

"Yes, you did, darlin.' You just don't remember. You was right there with mama when she passed, holdin' her hand. You was right there with her."

"I don't remember," Brenda said. "Why don't I remember?"

Ed Earl kept his explanation vague.

"Brenda, we had to put you in the hospital. All that time caring for Mama made you real sick, but you're all better now. It's gonna be okay. You're gonna be okay."

"How's daddy? Is he okay? What's he gonna do without Mama?" Brenda sensed that she was missing information, but a fog clouded her memory. No matter how hard she tried, she couldn't see through it. *Why can't I remember anything? I know mama was sick. I know I helped take care of her. I know we ate Christmas dinner together.* The thought of Christmas triggered a new response in Brenda.

"Daddy's fine," Ed Earl was saying.

Brenda Lee jumped up from her chair and went straight to the kitchen drawer where her mama had kept her yellow apron, the one with faded pink flowers on it. She pulled out the apron, hung it around her neck and tied it around her waist.

"Mama wants me to take care of him," she said.

Brenda didn't know where that thought came from, why she tied the apron on, or how she would do it, but she knew this was her charge. *Daddy needs me. Mama told me to take care of him. That's what I'm gonna do.* She would take care of her daddy for the rest of his life.

Ed Earl told Robert and their daddy that they shouldn't ever mention Brenda's nervous breakdown or the treatment that brought her out of it.

"People won't understand, and she don't need this life to be any harder on her," he had said.

Leroy and Robert had agreed, and there it was. They would never share their secret, and Brenda would be protected from the sad, troubling truth for as long as they were alive.

CHAPTER 29
A NEW SEASON, 1982

The very first sign that the South is transitioning from summer to fall is the light. Almost overnight, it seems, the angle of the sun changes. Morning light is cooler even before the weather is. The sky takes on a slightly deeper shade of blue and the morning shadows are longer. The dappled light through still-green leaves is cooler as well. In summer, the light is bright white, amplifying the heat, giving a visual reflection of the temperature. In September, the light softens to a gentle gold, hinting at the weather on the way.

The second sign of transition is the plastic-letter announcement on the sign at West Oaks Elementary School declaring that students could find out whose class they were assigned to for the upcoming school year starting Wednesday.

It had been two decades since Brenda had been in school, but she still loved seeing all the school supplies stocked in the stores. The big stacks of notebook paper, No. 2 pencils, the enormous 64-count boxes of crayons, protractors, compasses and three-ring notebooks made her feel plumb giddy inside. She used to love walking over to the school to see the printed class lists taped to the window of the lobby.

"Where's third grade?" one kid would ask.

"Over here, over here!" another would reply.

Brenda remembered checking the list when she was in third grade.

"I'm not in Miss Kerr's class." Brenda told her mama, reading each name carefully in search of her own. "Oh! I'm in Mrs. Lewis's class!" She jumped up and down, clapping her hands. She had wanted to be in Miss Kerr's class. Robert had been in her class, and she liked the idea of Robert paving the way for her, but Brenda loved the idea of school so much that she'd have been just as happy if they'd told her she'd been assigned to the lunchroom.

There was something simple and satisfying about being able to look at the list and knowing your place in the world. What she wouldn't give for a typed list on a piece of paper to tell her where she should be.

Even with her life interrupted so completely, Brenda couldn't help but feel the same sense of optimism that always seemed to come with school starting back and the promise of fall on the horizon.

Some people think of January as a fresh start. Others look to the Spring, but ever since she had started first grade, Brenda had thought of the fall as the time of new beginnings.

"Don't you just love this time of year?" she said to Miss Edna on their way home from the grocery store.

"I do love the cooler weather."

"I do too, but I mean don't you just love school startin' back? All those kids get to meet their new teachers and be with their friends again. I just love watching little Henry and Shelby get off the bus in the afternoons, so excited to show their mama what they did at school that day. I used to love doing that." The look on Brenda's face was wistful.

Autumn brings with it a sense of anticipation that starts with the homeroom question. From there it's waiting outside for the yellow school bus. Then it's pep rallies, football and homecoming. Somewhere in there is the hopeful expectation of the leaf change. There were maple trees all over Sumner. The display of yellow, red and orange leaves made the whole town glow for a few weeks in October, and not long after that came Halloween and the school and church fall festivals.

Fall was definitely Brenda's favorite season. She liked watching traffic slow down behind the buses with their red lights flashing. She liked hearing the marching band practice in the distance, and though she didn't understand a thing in the world about football, she loved nothing more than going to the West Oaks games on Friday nights and seeing the line of new drivers cruising up and down Maple Avenue after the home games. It reminded her of her younger days in a good kind of way.

The sign at the school had encouraged Brenda. It was time to turn over a new leaf. Of course, she'd still be working at the mill, and she'd keep taking care of daddy and Robert. She liked the way her hair looked, so she didn't imagine she'd ask Teresa to change her hair style. The supper menu at home was set in stone, so she didn't expect anything different there, and Brenda found comfort in that predictability. Still, change was coming. This fall was going to be a new beginning for her. She could feel it in her bones.

Tuesday after supper, Brenda drained the water from the pinto beans that been soaking all day on the stove. She then refilled the pot and seasoned the beans with a good bit of salt, some pepper and a ham bone, then covered the lid for them to simmer over low flames. The beans would be just about done by bedtime, when she would put them in the refrigerator to let them set overnight. Then, when she got home from work on Wednesday, she would start on the cornbread. She baked the cornbread in a metal pan that her mama had always used. The once-silver pan was now black, embossed with a repeated sunburst pattern that, when the cornbread was crispy, formed the same pattern on the dark brown crust. Her mama had always cooked cornbread in that pan instead of the iron skillet because the men of the house liked to eat the corners, where you got crust on the top and two-sides of the bread, making for an extra crunchy experience. Mama would usually leave the last corner for Brenda, but when her health started going down, Brenda made sure that her mama had the last corner. She deserved to have three sides of crunch.

    Pinto beans and cornbread were the staple Wednesday night dinner because her mama, and now Brenda herself, could cook them ahead of time. That meant that on Wednesdays, all she had to do was reheat the beans while the cornbread was cooking. Once the cornbread was done, and everybody had cleaned up and rested, the beans would be ready, leaving just enough time to eat before Ed Earl drove up to take her to church.

    For the first time since her stay at Eubanks County Hospital, Brenda was looking forward to church. Now that school was starting and fall was getting close, she was ready to worship like she used to.

The song leader picked "Power in the Blood" to kick off the service, and Brenda didn't hesitate to join in.

"There is power, power, wonder-working power,
In the blood of the Lamb.
There is power, power, wonder-working power,
In the precious blood of the Lamb."

Brenda sang the chorus with all the enthusiasm she could muster, which was plenty. She made the word "power" a single syllable:

"There is pyre, pyre, wonder-working pyre,
In the blood of the Lamb!
There is pyre, pyre, wonder-working pyre,
In the precious blood of the Lamb!"

Brother Alan slowed it down for the second song, but the words had both Ed Earl and Brenda in tears. "Because He Lives" had been their mama's favorite, and even though she'd been laid to rest years before, Brenda and Ed Earl could hear their mama's sweet voice singing the lyrics with her family in the pew by her side.

Ed Earl took to the pulpit, and Brenda was hanging on every word as if she didn't know how the gospel story ended.

"Because He Lives," Ed Earl started, still wiping away tears. "You know, there are days when I don't much feel like facing the next day, Brother David. There are days when I'm filled with fear, you know?"

"That was my mama's favorite song. I remember her singing it in the little church we grew up in, and I remember her singing it when her feeble little body was laying in that ol' hospital bed." Ed Earl was squalling. "But Sister Brenda, you know why that was her favorite song? I know you do. It's because she knew her hope wasn't in this life. No sir. Her hope was in glory!

"Do you know why, hah, brothers and sisters? She knew the Lord. He lived in her heart. When this ol' world let her down, hah, her Lord was there.

"Hah, when her neighbors, hah, disappointed her, hah, her Lord was there."

"Amen, brother!"

"When the Great Depression hit, hah, and it looked like she was gonna starve, hah, her Lord was there, hah!"

"Hallelujah!"

"And, when my mama's poor old, wore-out body took its last breath, I want you to know He was there. He was there! Hah! He was there! Hah! Because He lives! He was there!"

Voices from the congregation responded with affirmations.

"Yes!"

"Praise the Lord!"

"Thank you, Jesus!"

"Hallelujah!"

Ed Earl settled down and got real quiet. So did his little congregation.

"Because He lives, we have hope for tomorrow. This ol' hopeless world of ours is temporary. Things rust. Moths eat our clothes. Even the denim made at the mill wears out eventually, but Jesus don't wear out. I'm a-tellin' you, he never gets tired. He just stands at the door of our hearts, knocking.

"Won't you let him in? Won't you let him heal your hurt? Won't you let him take away your pain?

Brother Alan made his way back up to the front.

"Just as I am without one plea,
But that Thy blood was shed for me.
And, that Thou bidst me 'Come to Thee,'
O Lamb of God, I come. I come."

Brenda started walking toward the front. Tears were streaming down her face. Ed Earl met her at the altar. He hugged his sister as she began to sob. Several of the ladies from the church gathered around her. Laying their hands on her back and shoulders, they prayed out loud.

"Bless her Lord!"

"Bless her, Jesus!"

"Touch her, Lord."

Brenda's shoulders shook, and the tears poured. Ed Earl sobbed along with her. Brother Alan had moved on to "Amazing Grace" by the time Brenda could speak. Ed Earl still had his arms wrapped around his sister. She spoke directly into his ear.

"I'm ready for a new start, Ed Earl. I want the Lord to heal my broken heart. I want Him to make me happy again."

"I know. I know, Sister. I know."

After the service, Ed Earl and Mary Jo drove Brenda home.

"Ed Earl, I'm sorry for causing y'all to worry about me," she said.

"Honey, you don't have to apologize to me. You was sick, and that Cur-" Ed Earl stopped himself from saying his name. "You was taken advantage of."

"It's okay, you can say his name, Ed Earl. Curtis didn't take advantage of me," Brenda said. "I knew what I was doing. I just wanted somebody to love me like you love Mary Jo."

Mary Jo turned toward her sister-in-law, reached back and patted her leg with her hand.

"Brenda Lee. I know you thought Curtis was the one for you, but I want you to know he's not," Mary Jo said. "The Lord may have somebody out there for you, Honey, but I don't think it's Curtis Whitfield. You know your mama and daddy never did care for him."

"I know they didn't," Brenda said. "But I feel like y'all didn't know him like I know him. Y'all don't see the good in people that I see."

"Bless your heart, you have always seen the good in people," Mary Jo said. "We just think this time, you wanted to see good where they wasn't none."

"Maybe," Brenda said, she sat quietly for a couple of miles before speaking again.

"Tonight, I felt like the Lord gave me a brand-new start, you know, kinda like the first day of school. I'm not sad anymore. It's just like you said, Ed Earl. He took my burden off me."

"Hallelujah!" Ed Earl said. "That's what my Jesus does."

"I feel like I can go home and take care of daddy and Robert, and them not worry about me."

"Praise the Lord," Mary Jo said. "Brenda, Honey, you know you can call me if you ever want to talk, don't you?"

"I know," Brenda said. "I don't want to be a bother. Y'all know I don't remember much about it, but I know how y'all took care of me, daddy and Robert after mama died."

"Honey, we love you," Ed Earl said. "You're family."

They had pulled onto Avenue D.

"Ed Earl, do you reckon mama is looking down on us from heaven?" Brenda asked. It was a question that had been burning in her mind for the past few weeks. *What would mama have thought about me hitchhiking my way to Tennessee? I wouldn't want to embarrass her in front of St. Peter.*

"I don't rightly know, Brenda," Ed Earl said. "I mean, on the one hand, there ain't no tears in heaven. I can't imagine somebody up there in perfection looking down on the mess we live in down here without crying.

"On the other hand, the Bible says we have guardian angels. I can imagine that an angel might report back to mama on how we're doing."

"Lord, I hope not," Brenda said. "I think she'd be mad at me for the way I've been acting."

"Brenda, anger is a sin," Ed Earl said. "And that means there ain't no anger in heaven. So, I can guarantee that mama hasn't been angry with you. Now, she might have pled your cause before the Good Lord, but I just don't believe she could be angry."

"Thank you for saying that Ed Earl." He had stopped the car at the front gate to the mill house. "Y'all gonna get out?" Brenda said. "I've got some pinto beans and cornbread."

"No, Sugar. We need to get on back to the house. Sister Thompson is having surgery in the morning, and I want to be up at the hospital when they take her back."

Brenda loved that about her brother. If somebody was having surgery. He was there. If there was a death in a family, Ed Earl was sitting beside them. If there was teen-ager making a bad mistake, her brother was talking to his mama. He was the least selfish person she knew, including Miss Edna.

"Well, I guess I'll see you Sunday. Y'all take care."

Brenda got out of the car and walked up the steps to the front porch. Her brother waited until she was inside, and the door had closed behind her before driving off. That's what Ed Earl did. He always made sure people were safe before he left them.

CHAPTER 30
HOMECOMING

Midway through October, just as the leaves reach their peak, Sumner itself reaches its own gold and white climax. Teenage girls begin shopping for formals and stylish dresses while their dates search for suits that fit and ties that match the girls' outfits. Orders for mum corsages and rose boutonnieres come in daily at Johnette's Flowers, and hay bales and mums pop up in every store front. It's homecoming weekend, and all of Sumner is a part of it.

Brenda was never on the homecoming court and never went to a homecoming dance, but she wouldn't miss a homecoming parade or the big game for anything in the world. Much like the Fourth of July parade, the homecoming procession starts at the school and ends at the mill, collecting in the parking lot of First Baptist Church, not far from the West Oaks Mill's big smokestacks. And because everything in Sumner revolves around mill life, the school plans the parade so that all the first- and second-shift workers at the mill can see it and none of them miss their shift.

Every girl on the homecoming court rides on the back of a convertible, steadying herself by planting her high-heeled feet in the backseat as she waves at the crowd gathered on the roadside. Just in case you don't know the girls, which isn't likely in a town the size of Sumner, every girl has her name spelled out in glitter letters on a poster board on each side of the car. The homecoming parade fills out with flatbed trucks decorated by school clubs, and every cheerleader and football player from peewee to varsity, along with the marching band in the procession. The drum corps provides a steady beat for the parade to march to, and twice along the route, the whole band bursts into the homecoming theme song.

After the parade, everybody, except the 3-11 shift workers, darts home to get ready for the game. The mill never stops weaving denim, but you can bet that if a second-shift mill employee has a son on the football team or a daughter on the homecoming court, another worker will volunteer to switch shifts so they can go to the game. That's just what people do in Sumner.

For those who can't come, the local radio station always broadcasts the game, and the mill bosses allow workers to keep their radios on, to catch what they can of the action on the field. Every once in a while, you'll hear a whoop or a holler after Dan Houston announces a first down, a good tackle or a touchdown.

"Go boys!"

"Get him!"

"Touchdown!"

Every parent, grandparent, sibling, teacher and former teacher comes out to the West Oaks football stadium for the Friday night homecoming game. Joining them in the stands are former cheerleaders who cheer on the Dragons from their seats, and former football players, a few of whom can still fit into their letter jackets, snug or not. And there's always a bevy of past homecoming queens and their courts who come back to watch the current year's royalty take their walks down the 50-yard line.

Brenda always loved going to the games, and this year was no exception. She sat in the stands and waved at friends, neighbors and church acquaintants. And sure enough, there was an autumn breeze that blew across, sending the first chill of the year up her back. She sat on the edge of her seat so she could see the pretty girls all dressed up in their evening gowns.

"Look at her!" Brenda exclaimed, elbowing the person next to her. "She's just beautiful. Do you know who her mama was?"

Her seat neighbor didn't respond. She just nodded and kept watching, listening for the loudspeaker to announce the next girl's name.

"That dress is so sparkly!" Brenda said too loudly. "I bet it cost $500!"

This continued as all eight of the homecoming court members were called to the field. Brenda listened to all the details the announcer read, hoping to catch the name of somebody she went to high school with.

"That's Kathy's daughter!" she said to her neighbor. "I went to school with her!"

Brenda tended to forget that the person sitting beside her probably went to school with Kathy as well, and if not, he or she surely went to school with Kathy's husband. Still, it was exciting to find a connection to the court.

When it was time to announce the name of the homecoming queen, the whole stadium grew quiet with anticipation.

"And your 1982 homecoming queen is Autumn Bates!"

As soon as the announcer spoke the girl's name, the crowd erupted with applause and a standing ovation. Brenda was the hardest clapper and loudest supporter.

"Whoop! Ain't she just beautiful!" Brenda said, her applause as enthusiastic as her voice. "She's just perfect!"

There's no doubt about it, homecomings are special in Sumner, and this year's felt extra special for Brenda.

The Dragons won their homecoming game, defeating the Devils from Paris, and that was the cherry on top of an already sweet night. After the game, everybody in the stands went down to the field to congratulate the players, the queen, the court, the band, the coaches and each other. The parking lot didn't clear out until after the mill whistle blew, marking the end of the second shift. Laney, who had swapped shifts so she could help Henry and Shelby get ready for the parade, brought Brenda home, so she wouldn't have to walk now that the temperature had dropped.

Brenda tried to be quiet as she entered the house. Her daddy and Robert were already asleep. She never understood why they didn't like going to the homecoming game. Robert said one time that he didn't like reliving memories. She didn't understand that either. Brenda liked high school. She wasn't the prettiest or smartest or most popular or anything, but there was something about those four years at West Oaks High that made her smile.

CHAPTER 31
HAIRSPRAY AND SOUTHERN LIVING

Homecoming lasts all weekend in Sumner. The homecoming dance is held on the Saturday after the game, so there's a whole other day dedicated to getting ready, taking pictures, eating out at a nice restaurant in Paris and dancing with your date. The getting ready part impacted Brenda and Miss Edna.

Miss Edna came to pick Brenda up for their beauty shop appointment a little early and honked the horn.

Brenda hurried to the car.

"Is something the matter?" Brenda said, breathless from the near jog to the car.

"Nothin's wrong," Miss Edna said. "It's homecoming you know. The shop will be full with the regulars and on top of that there will be a bunch of teenagers in there waiting to get their hair fixed for tonight."

"I don't mind waiting on them, Miss Edna," Brenda said. "I like listening to them talk about their dresses and their dates."

"Oh, I like it too, but I don't want to be stuck there all day," Miss Edna replied. "I've got work of my own that I need to do."

"Did you go to the game last night? I did," Brenda announced. "The homecoming court was just beautiful!"

"Yeah, we went," Miss Edna said. "They was pretty, but can you tell me when dresses got that tight? My mama would've hog-tied me before she'd let me out of the house wearing something like that. It's just not proper."

In the background Swap Shop was coming on the radio.

"Congratulations to the West Oak Dragons on their win over the Paris Devils at last night's homecoming game!" Mike said. "Now let's get on to our show. Welcome to Swap Shop, what do you have to give or what do you need?"

"Mike, I'm looking for somebody who might have lost a class of '56 class ring at last night's football game."

"Turn that up, Miss Edna!" Brenda said.

"You found a class ring?" Mike asked the caller.

"Yes sir, I did. It's a class of 1956 class ring from West Oaks High. It's got a ruby-red stone in it."

"Is it a boy's ring or a girl's ring?" Mike asked.

"It looks like it's a girls ring, Mike."

"Alright listeners, if you're a member of the West Oaks class of 1956 and you had a class ring with a red stone in it, call the station and we'll connect you to the finder."

"What year did you graduate?" Miss Edna asked Brenda.

"I graduated in 1956!" Brenda said. "I don't know where my class ring is. I haven't worn it in I don't know how long."

"Could it be yours?"

"Well, I don't know. I guess I need to look and see if I can find mine."

The girls finished their conversation as they walked in the door of a bustling Lords and Ladies. Every seat was taken. Some teen-age girls were sitting in the floor. The level of the chatter was nearly deafening.

"Hey ladies!" Tally said to Brenda and Miss Edna. "Girls, can I get a couple of you to give up your seats so these ladies can rest until it's your turn?"

"Yes ma'am!" said a perky blonde in a ponytail. She was fresh faced and dressed in a button-down shirt too big for her. Her friend, a brunette with wavy hair and dark eyes, stood up as well, making way for Brenda and Miss Edna.

"It's gonna be a minute, girls. Get you a magazine and take a seat, OK?" Tally said.

Miss Edna picked up an old copy of *Guideposts* and started thumbing her way through it. She didn't know if she'd have time to finish one story or the whole magazine, so she started at the front.

Brenda found an October edition of *Southern Living*. The magazine cover is what caught her eye. Orange and gold maple leaves filled the shiny cover from top to bottom. The trees lined a leaf-covered sidewalk. It reminded her of Sumner and exactly captured how Brenda liked to picture this time of year. The lead article was *Where to Find The South's Fall Color,* and Brenda thought to herself, *They ought to come right here to Sumner.*

Tally was working on her first of three girls going to the homecoming dance. They all needed to come early because they had to get their makeup done, then get their pictures made, then go out to eat in Paris before coming back to Sumner for the dance.

Brenda had quit looking at her magazine and instead eavesdropped on the girl's conversation. One of them said her dress still wasn't ready.

"Whoop!" Brenda said too loudly. She caught herself, but she couldn't help wondering what that poor girl was gonna do if her dress wasn't ready. She was far too pretty to wear a gunny sack. Brenda laughed at herself. *That girl wouldn't even know what a gunny sack was.*

After about an hour's wait, Teresa called Brenda over to the reclining shampoo chair. The shampoo was her favorite part, and Teresa was about the best shampooer she'd ever seen. She always lathered twice and massaged her head real good, and she was always real careful not to get Brenda's shirt wet when she rinsed out the shampoo. She could just lay back in that chair all day.

With her hair washed and wrapped in a towel, Teresa went back to one of the teenagers she was working on. Her hair was a work of art. Teresa had rolled it up in hot rollers, combed it out and teased it real big. She made the girl's bangs go way up high and then fall just over her eyebrows. On each side, she sprayed the girl's hair into a cowlick. Teresa told the girl she was too pretty to hide her face. Cowlicks on both sides would frame her face with her pretty blond hair, she told her. Once done, Teresa enveloped her customer in a cloud of hair spray.

"Hold your breath, Hon!" she said. "We don't want this to go anywhere."

Brenda had complete faith that when the girl woke up tomorrow, her hair would look exactly like it did right then.

"Lord, I wish I had that head full of hair!" Brenda said to Teresa and the girl. "It's so pretty. You should've been the homecoming queen."

The girl thanked her and Teresa and walked out the door like she was ready for Hollywood.

"Ok, Brenda, come on over here, and let's get your hair up in rollers," Teresa told her. Teresa expertly rolled Brenda's hair in 5 minutes flat. She had the dryer hot and waiting on her.

"Only 50 minutes behind," Teresa said. "I can make that up!"

"Don't hurry too much, now, I want my hair to last all week!" Brenda hollered at her from beneath the dryer hood.

"Don't you worry, Sugar," Teresa hollered back. "You're gonna look like *you* should be the homecoming queen!"

"Whoop! That'd be the day!" Brenda yelled over the dryer. Brenda smiled and kept smiling as she looked through her magazine while her hair dried. She normally would try to talk to Pat, Peg, Jane Ellen or Miss Edna while she sat there with her hair under a hood, but not today. She was enjoying Teresa's compliment and half listening to the homecoming girls talk about their dresses and their dates. And, when she wasn't eavesdropping, she was thinking about church and her promise to the Good Lord to turn over a new leaf.

  While Brenda and Miss Edna were drying, two more homecoming girls got their hair fixed for the dance. The first girl, a pretty brunette, got hers in an up-do, a 6-inch-tall twist of curls and lacquer with tendrils in front of each of her ears and bangs half as tall as the rest of her hair. Teresa was pleased with her masterpiece. The other girl had short black hair that Tally curled and teased until it looked like she had twice as much hair as she had started with. It really was amazing to see what those girls could accomplish with a curling iron, hairspray and a teasing comb.

CHAPTER 32
FLIPPING THE MATTRESS

Brenda and Miss Edna were about 30 minutes later than usual when they got in the car to head home–all-in-all not too bad with that kind of traffic at the beauty shop.

"I should have mentioned that ring from Swap Shop," Miss Edna said. "Somebody in there might have heard something about a lost class ring."

"I didn't even think about it," Brenda said, "or I would have said something."

"Oh well."

"Oh well."

The women rode the rest of the way to the mill village in silence, Miss Edna thankful for the quiet, and Brenda lost in a homecoming reverie.

"Thank you, Miss Edna," Brenda said as she exited the Buick.

"You're welcome, Hon."

Inside the house, Brenda went to the bathroom to check her hair in the mirror. She liked to see it freshly done, with no lint in it. She knew it was near lunch time, but she wasn't hungry yet, and neither her daddy nor Robert were at home.

Instead, Brenda went to her bedroom and begin rummaging through her dresser drawers in search of her class ring.

She remembered the day she got it like it was yesterday. The ring came like the Christmas presents that always seemed to have miraculously appeared. The Branches didn't have the kind of extra money laying around that would buy an expensive class ring.

"What did you call it?" her daddy had asked when Brenda had brought it up at the supper table.

"It's a class ring, daddy. Everybody gets one before they graduate. You get to choose what kind of stone you want in it, I want a ruby, and they put the year you're graduating on it. They're real pretty, and everybody I know is getting one."

"Is that true Ed Earl? Robert?" her daddy asked.

Robert didn't reply, but Ed Earl did.

"Yes sir. Just about all the girls are getting them. Some of the boys too."

"Boys get 'em too," Brenda said. "The way you know a girl is going steady with a boy is when she wears his class ring on her finger."

"How much does a ring like that cost, Hon," asked Brenda's mama, putting her rough hand on top of Brenda's.

"Well, I don't rightly know, but it's not a real ruby, mama, so it can't be that much!" Brenda said with excitement.

Brenda knew that when her mama spoke up in a conversation, Leroy would be more understanding, and before the night was up, Brenda was ordering her class ring with a ruby-red stone.

That had been so long ago, and Brenda couldn't remember the last time she had worn her ring. Mill workers don't wear jewelry. Too much could go wrong with something on your finger. A loose ring could get caught on a gear, and that would be bad news. One man had died in the mill years before when his hand got caught in a machine, someone had told her. It drug him into the carder, and he couldn't get loose.

So, Brenda kept her jewelry in the top drawer in a wooden jewelry box her mama had gotten one year with her Green Stamps.

Inside was her mama's wedding ring, a cameo that one of her aunts had given her, a charm bracelet that had been a birthday gift years ago, and there it was! Her class ring. She tried to slide it on, but the toll of age and mill work only allowed it to go as far as her second finger joint. She held her hand out to admire the ring that suddenly looked much smaller than she remembered. She removed the ring and placed it back in her jewelry box, smiling at the memory.

Having confirmed the Swap Shop ring wasn't hers, Brenda shifted her worries to the owner of the class ring. *Does she even know it's missing? If it means as much to her as mine does to me, well, I'd just be beside myself.*

Brenda caught herself before getting too worked up. Any other time, she would have grabbed her yearbook and looked through all the seniors wondering if she should call each one and ask them about the ring. *I don't have to do that.*

"Old things have passed away," Brenda said out loud to herself, quoting something she had remembered Ed Earl read out of the Bible.

She took the bedspread, quilts, sheets and pillowcases off her bed for washing. Then she single-handedly flipped and turned her mattress before remaking the bed in fresh sheets that smelled like sunshine and clean air from drying on the clothesline out back. *Mama used to flip the mattress at the change of every season. I need to make sure I remember to do that.*

"All things are made new!" Brenda said, continuing the verse from memory.

After remaking the bed and putting the sheets in the washing machine, Brenda decided it was time for another change. Perhaps prompted by homecoming and class rings, or maybe realizing that the summer had robbed her happiness, Brenda had a sudden hankering for a hamburger. *I want a hamburger and French fries for supper!*

For every Saturday for as long as she could remember supper had been meatloaf made from ground beef served with a helping of mashed potatoes and peas. She never did like meatloaf or peas. *I think I'm gonna flip this ol' mattress!*

Brenda went to the kitchen and reached for her mother's yellow apron but caught herself. There had always been other aprons to choose from, but Brenda could never bring herself to wear a different one.

She selected a pretty blue apron folded into the drawer for so long that it was permanently creased. Brenda tied the apron around her waist, took the ground beef from the refrigerator and began making hamburger patties. The patties formed, she cut the potatoes into strips for French fries. The peas stayed in the freezer. *We can have 'em later.*

Brenda went to the door and saw Henry playing in his mama's yard.

"Henry, can you ask your mama if I can borrow some hamburger buns, Hon? If you do, I just might have an Oreo in the cabinet for you!"

"Yes ma'am!" Henry said, running inside. He was back in a flash with hamburger buns.

"You tell your mama I'll replace these when I go to the grocery store next week, OK?" Brenda told him as she handed him two Oreos. "You make sure to give one to Shelby."

CHAPTER 33
HAMBURGER AND FRENCH FRIES

Leroy and Robert could tell something was different the minute they came in for supper.

"Supper's ready!" Brenda called out.

Brenda's daddy and brother washed their hands and sat down at the chrome dinette.

Brenda presented two plates, each holding a hamburger and a mound of fries.

"This ain't meatloaf," Leroy said, perturbed "What's…"

Brenda cut him off.

"No, it's hamburgers and French fries, Daddy," Brenda said. "I remembered that hamburger you and mama got me when I graduated and decided I'd like to have one."

"But we have meatloaf on Saturdays," Leroy said, still holding his fork in one hand and a butter knife in the other.

"We *used to* have meatloaf every Saturday," Brenda said. "Don't you think it's a good idea sometimes to do something out of the ordinary, to make a change."

"Now don't be gettin' any ideas, Brenda Lee," Leroy said. "Your last good idea 'bout killed us all!"

Brenda knew she was better when she realized that her daddy's words didn't sting as they might have before.

"Oh, Daddy, I ain't talking about leaving home," Brenda said. "We're just making a little change. It's still ground beef, and it's still potatoes. It's just cooked different. I just got to thinking how much I enjoyed that hamburger when I graduated high school, and I couldn't remember the last time I had one."

Brenda watched her brother for a reaction. Robert looked up at his sister, then at his daddy, his nose still pointed toward his plate.

"I like hamburgers too," he said, hesitating ever so slightly. He couldn't believe himself. For the first time in his life, he was agreeing with his hare-brained sister.

"See there!" Brenda said. "Y'all take a bite. You're gonna like it!"

Leroy shrugged his shoulders, laid his silverware down, lifted his burger and bit into it. He didn't say anything else about meatloaf.

The next morning on the way to church, Brenda had Ed Earl and Mary Jo laughing till they were in tears.

"I bet Daddy was fit to be tied when you handed him that plate!" Ed Earl said.

"I wasn't sure what he'd do," Brenda said. "I kept waiting for him to holler at me or dump it in the trash, but he didn't, Ed Earl! He just put down his fork, took that first bite, then another and another and kept right on eating until it was all gone. He never said a word, but he and Robert both cleared their plates. They didn't even mention meatloaf!"

At church that morning, Brenda sang with all the enthusiasm she could muster when Brother Alan led "Victory in Jesus."

"I heard about His healing,
"of His cleansing power revealing
"How He made the lame
"to walk again
"and 'caused the blind to see
"And then I cried,
"Dear Jesus,
"come and heal my
"broken spirit'
"And somehow Jesus came and brought to me the victory."

When the hymn ended, Ed Earl walked to the pulpit with a broad smile on his face.

"Brothers and sisters, I had planned to preach to y'all this morning about taking up your cross and following Jesus, but the Lord has gone and changed my mind.

"My sister told me a story this morning, and it left me with a question I'd like to ask you."

"Whoop!" Brenda said, quickly covering her mouth.

Ed Earl smiled.

"When was the last time you ate a hamburger?

"Now, I know that might seem like a silly question, but it ain't. It's one of the most important questions you'll ever answer.

"When was the last time you ate a hamburger?" Ed Earl paused, letting the question hang in the air, before resuming his sermon.

"You see, when the good Lord fed bread and fish to the 5,000, it didn't matter what they ate, you know. What mattered was who fed them. You've got to understand, it wasn't the disciples that fed them, hah. No sir. It wasn't the boy who had the bread and fish, hah. No ma'am.

"No, hah, the person that fed them was Jesus himself, hah, the bread of life, hah. The Son of God.

The one!" Ed Earl stopped for dramatic effect, then continued in a whisper.

"Who came to earth to change everything."

"Brothers and sisters, the biggest miracle you will ever see is the change in your heart when you make the decision to follow the Lord. But if all you did was talk about the Lord, if all you did was talk about change, hah. If all you did was tell people you had changed, but nobody ever saw a difference.

"Well, then, I don't reckon you changed.

"How many of you sitting here this morning said you were going to make a change in the new year, hah? How many of you, hah, are in a rut? How many, hah, of you have been eating bread and fish for years when the good Lord put hamburger on the menu?

"What if, hah, the Lord, told you to quit eating fish and start eating hamburger?

"Would you do it? Or would you keep on eating fish because that's what you've always done?

"It's time for a change."

Brenda Lee couldn't stop smiling. *I didn't perform no miracle,* she thought to herself. *All I did was make a hamburger. Now, here He is turning it into a sermon!*

After saying their goodbyes at church, Ed Earl and Mary Jo drove Brenda home.

"That was a good message!" Brenda told her brother.

"Yes, it was," Mary Jo agreed.

"Well, you inspired it, Brenda Lee," Ed Earl told her. "I'd give anything to have been a fly on the wall when you put that hamburger in front of daddy and Robert."

He chuckled again at the thought of Leroy expecting a slice of meatloaf with mashed potatoes, only to look down and see a hamburger and fries.

"Well, you inspired me, too, Ed Earl," Brenda replied. "When I get home today, I'm gonna clean out my closet. There's clothes in there that I've had 20 years. Today's the day I'm getting rid of them."

"Well, that sounds like good idea, Brenda Lee."

"I'd pass some your way Mary Jo, but I ain't never been as petite as you are, Hon!" Brenda said to her sister-in-law. "My clothes would swallow you

whole!"

After lunch, Brenda went to her bedroom, changed out of her church clothes, then stood in front of her open closet. *Got to keep going, I reckon,* Brenda thought to herself. She determined to toss anything that didn't fit or had a hole or stain in it. It was quick work.

She found sizes from 10 to 18 and was pleased that she could get rid of the biggest sizes as well as the smallest ones.

When she finished, she surveyed what remained. She was missing a few things. *Now where is my blouse with pale pink roses on it? And where are my pink pants? It's too cold to wear those clothes now, but I love that outfit, and I don't have...*

Brenda's mind stopped mid-thought.

Realizing where her favored ensemble was, Brenda's stomach suddenly feeling empty. *Lord, help me.* If she had looked in the mirror, Brenda would have seen the color gone from her face. *They're in my suitcase.*

More than four months had passed since Brenda had attempted to go to the World's Fair, suitcase in hand. Now, it felt like two lifetimes ago. She had found healing at the altar and given her heartbreak to Jesus, but the thought of the suitcase flooded her mind with thoughts she thought she had put behind her.

Brenda bent over and looked under her bed for the suitcase, unable to remember in the process whether she or someone else had put it there. *Maybe daddy, Robert or Mary Jo put it there when I came home from the hospital.* She pulled the suitcase from beneath her bed and hoisted it onto the mattress.

Brenda unlatched the bag and carefully opened it, then stared for a good minute at everything she had packed for her trip to see Curtis. Nothing was disturbed. On top was the roadmap she had taken from the glove compartment in Robert's car, carefully and methodically folded back together. Just under the map were her favorite pants and blouse, clean and ready for hanging in a Knoxville hotel room.

She ran her hand over the clothes. The suitcase's pale blue satin interior reminded her of the inside of a coffin. A chill ran up her back, and Brenda shivered. Her mama used to say a rabbit was running over her grave when that happened. She didn't like that feeling.

Well, I don't reckon I'll be wearing these anytime soon, she thought. *Maybe, I should just leave them here.*

Brenda closed the still-packed suitcase, latched it and slid it under her bed.

You never know. If we can eat hamburgers and French fries on a Saturday night, who knows what could happen next?

Lint Head

Acknowledgements

Complete and exhaustive thanks to Gregg Lewis. Your edits, your advice and your encouragement are the reason I finally decided to push forward with publishing *Lint Head*. You didn't have to, but you took time on your vacations and during your free time to read, make edits, call with suggestions, send emails and ask questions, and *Lint Head* is better for it.

A thousand thank yous to Karl Peters. Regardless of what wisdom teaches us, people *do* judge books by their covers, and I can't imagine trusting the cover of my first novel to anyone but you, the most talented designer I know.

Thanks also to Tommy Toles, former newspaper editor and my boss 25 years ago. It was your idea to have me write a regular column for the daily newspaper we worked at. Those columns helped me find my voice and no doubt influenced *Lint Head*.

Bill Fortenberry has written about and for other people for nearly 40 years. A former journalist and current public relations professional, he spent the first half of his career as a reporter, editor and columnist for his hometown daily newspaper. Since 2001, he has worked as a marketing and communications professional.

Bill grew up in the American South in a family "poor as dirt" but rich with stories and characters. It is the hearing of those stories that instilled a life-long appreciation for storytelling, especially those that inspire or make one laugh. He is husband to Lisa, an amazing artist and executive assistant; father to Ethan, a Nashville-based singer-songwriter; and father Autumn, a first-grade teacher.

You can read his blog, *Kudzudad,* where Bill muses about faith, family, friends and his own struggles with mental health at bfortenberry.com.

Made in the USA
Columbia, SC
26 July 2024

86fc4d9f-8f36-4000-b68b-c05b153ea24aR01